CASS TELL

THE SAVANT

a novel

destinée

The Savant - A Novel
CASS TELL

Published by Destinée Media www.destineemedia.com
Written by Cass Tell www.casstell.com
Cover concept by Per-Ole Lind www.perolelind.com

ISBN: 978-1-938367-38-0

TABLE OF CONTENTS

CHAPTER 1

At the top of the oak tree I had an eternal view of the world, but being wobbly, my foot slipped, and I lost my balance.

My left hand grabbed a small branch that held for a moment, and then it bent and broke, cracking like a pistol shot. Time stood still as my body tilted backward beyond the point of control, this followed by acceleration with pointed green leaves zipping past my face, my hands flailing to grab anything, while thick branches hit my legs and chest.

I bounced against the tree trunk, its rough bark biting into my arm and chest and suddenly a large rock on the ground greeted my head with a hard *whop*.

Everything went black.

It's not certain what happened after that, but sometime later I woke up on my bed and through the haze, I heard my grandfather and Uncle Louie talking.

"Darn kid could-a killed his-self," My grandfather said.

"Think he'll wake up?" Louie asked.

"He better. He's all we got unless you get married and make me some grandkids."

"Marriage ain't for me," Louie replied.

"Then we better hope to heaven he'll make it."

There was silence, as though they left the room, and then Louie proclaimed, "He's a simpleton, ain't he. The school don't want him. Count it up, for seven years now he's been uneducated, floating around this place. Neither of us can control him."

"Sometimes he's like an Oklahoma twister," my grandfather stated.

"More like the village-idiot," Louie remarked. "Creepy, that wide-eyed stare. Remember that first day we got him, that little kid with the big blue eyes and lonely face?"

"It was like he was lost in a daydream."

"More like a vacuum in his head," Louie pronounced.

"I know. What're we gonna do with him?"

"Maybe stick him in one of those places. Might stop him from killin' his-self."

"You mean an insane asylum?" my grandfather asked.

"Yeah, a crazy house. It'd be the best thing."

My eyes slightly opened, and I saw my grandfather with his hands in the pockets of his bib overalls. "What's an asylum?" I asked.

Louie's face lit up. "Well, I'll be. He might make it."

The pain in my legs and chest was a hundred times worse than when the neighbor's dog bit me on the hand. My head pounded, and the room spun around like a carousel.

They ignored me and debated the pros and cons of this special-home place, but the *asylum* word wasn't used anymore.

As they talked, something unusual and not easy to describe was happening. In my hazy mind, their words appeared as contours and hues. It was something like colorful clouds forming shapes, merging together into rivers. The rivers didn't flow in straight lines but curved and bent, each word forming the next part upstream. That made me dizzy and nauseous.

Confused, I tried to sit up, but my grandfather's steady hand pushed me back onto the bed.

* * *

Later that day I considered getting up, yet the world continued to spin. I figured it would take a while to get back to normal, although I often heard people say I wasn't normal, like teachers at school.

Having to pee real bad, I moved my hands across my ribs to examine the pain, and then slowly got up and walked to the bathroom. Looking down at the toilet, something was unusual. My pee looked different. Instead of a steady stream, it was like millions of small golden droplets connected together.

When finished in the bathroom, I limped through my grandfather's house, and everything had changed. Details were everywhere that hadn't been there before like cracks in the old lampshades and on the wooden floor. The worn brown couch in the living room was now a mix of auburn and grays. All shapes and colors of furniture in the house were different, their particulars distinct and unreal.

That evening I was up and around, and after dinner, we did what we always did. We sat on the front porch, and Louie and my grandfather sipped whiskey, and they argued about cars. Louie said Fords were the best and grandfather argued for Chevys. They had a million reasons why one was better than the other.

Another thing they did was to guess cars. We lived on a small farm, twenty acres of dry California earth covered with orange trees. A narrow country road went by our place, and it disappeared over the hill about three miles to the west.

When a car came over the hill, Louie and my grandfather guessed what kind it was, first by looking at the headlights and then when they heard the motor. They bet a penny on each car, and most of the time they were wrong, so not much money was exchanged.

In the distance, a car came over the hill, and Louie said, "That's a fifty-two Ford."

"No way," Grandfather said. "It's a forty-eight Chevy."

I never got involved in car guessing, regularly just sitting there rocking back and forth. This time I noticed a subtle pink glow around the headlights. Then I saw a light that mushroomed into a shape that was somewhat like a pink river flowing toward us. At a certain point the river dissipated into something like bubbles and waterdrops.

"It's a nineteen-fifty Studebaker," I said.

Louie laughed

My grandfather grinned and said, "You're way off, kid."

"Ain't so," I countered.

Shortly after, the car passed us, and it was just as I had claimed, a pink, nineteen fifty Studebaker.

"Well, I'll be darned," Louie said. "The kid got lucky."

Somehow, it didn't seem like luck.

For the next half hour, I correctly guessed eight out of the following eleven cars and then hobbled off to bed, my body so sore I could hardly move.

After putting my aching head on the pillow, I couldn't sleep. Instead, images kept sweeping across my room, the shapes of headlights and the colors of car-bodies, innumerable shades of pinks and blues and greens It was like being inside a kaleidoscope.

As the lights and colors swirled around me, I reveled in this new and fascinating experience.

Then I had a reasoned thought. I actually didn't know that much about cars, except what I had absorbed from Louie and my grandfather. So, how had I won the guessing-game?

That needed some figuring out.

CHAPTER 2

That was the first time I ever won a game, and it made me profoundly curious. My grandfather said it was blind luck, but somehow it seemed more than that. The question was where this ability came from?

So, during the days after the fall from the tree, all my thoughts focused on car-guessing. I had plenty of time to think, mainly because it was hard to move around.

It wasn't easy to get out of bed in the mornings as my head and arm and back were in deep pain. It was not easy to do the simplest tasks like spreading peanut butter on my bread or brushing my teeth.

I suspected that I'd never freely move again and wondered if Louie and my grandfather should have taken me to the hospital.

Louie had poked me in my ribs, and said, "Ain't nothing broke, it seems."

My grandfather replied, "Even if there was, kids naturally mend themselves, so we can save on the doctor bill."

I reckoned they knew what they were talking about, so just needed to be patient to get back my usual self. Before the fall I couldn't stay still no matter how hard I tried, with quick jerky movements in everything I did. Now I moved like a slow worm.

At school, teachers said I was overactive, whatever that meant? In fact, that's what got me sent home most of the time, saying I was impossible to educate and a disruption to the other students.

Once I was sitting outside the principal's office, and Uncle Louie was inside, and they were talking. While waiting there, my hand went up and down and up and down, my pointy finger touching my knee and then my forehead, over and over, keeping a constant rhythm. I hummed along with the movement.

Through the door, I heard Uncle Louie ask, "So, what's wrong with the kid?"

The principal replied, "Mister Harken, I don't mean to alarm you, but it's like he's in another world. He doesn't seem to notice what's going on."

"What do you mean?"

"His teacher says he stares into space, oblivious to what's going on around him. He rarely speaks to anyone."

"Yeah, I know," Louie replied. Anything else?"

"Yes, there is. He gets into these repetitive actions, for instance, touching his head and then his desk. It's extremely disruptive for the other students. They think it's funny."

"I'll take him home," Louie stated.

"That might be the best thing. We could try and help you by arranging an evaluation with a specialist."

"Don't worry. Me and his grandfather will take care of it."

As they talked, my mind drifted off for I wasn't sure why repetitions were a problem? They seemed the best thing to do. When teachers got boring, which was most of the time, it was natural to tap my head or click a pencil against the desk.

On the farm, my favorite repetition was to run barefoot on a path through the orange trees to the back of our property where I touched the trunk of the tall oak tree. Then I'd sprint back and touch the exterior wall of our house and then back to the oak tree, and do it again and again.

When running, most of the time I could pretty much go in a straight line. Ambling slowly was entirely different, as that's when I got unsteady.

Once a week Uncle Louie took me to the city swimming pool where instructors taught spastic kids how to swim. There were three other children in my swimming class, and they had difficulty to walk, and the teachers held them up in the water, so they wouldn't drown.

I was different, not needing to be held. Quickly I learned to swim, and from then on, I'd go from one end of the pool to the other, back and forth. When I reached the side, I'd slap the blue tile three times, spit in the runoff gutter that paralleled the edge of the pool, and then swim back to the other end and tap and spit.

Uncle Louie often sat on the side of the pool to watch the teenagers jumping off the diving board. He also smiled at women, and they laughed back. Then, he'd go to the high dive and when everyone was watching he'd do a double flip, and people clapped.

I didn't look at him too much because my mind was focused on swimming to the wall and tapping the tile and spitting. I'd do that thirty or forty times in a row, or even more.

When swimming, the teenagers got out of my way often laughing and saying, "Look out for the little spastic."

Sometimes they'd splash water on my face like they were trying to keep me away from them, but I didn't really notice because my concentration was on touching the wall.

One day after the fall, when moving was more comfortable, I shuffled down the dirt path to the oak tree. But, when I got to the tree I couldn't touch it.

As my finger got close to the tree trunk, my body vibrated, and yellow electricity emanated from the entire tree like someone had turned on a fluorescent light. Then I got distracted by the tree's thick bark with its endless contours and deep gullies. It was like each gully was a world of its own.

For a long time, I watched red fire ants scurry along a trail at the base of the tree. But, no matter how hard I tried I couldn't touch the tree.

That caused my body to tremble even more, for I was suddenly confronted by a reality. By not touching the tree, it meant I couldn't complete a repetition that was such a central part of my life, the back and forth from the tree to the house.

When I looked closer at the yellow electricity, I saw fingers coming toward me, like tentacles. It was as though the tree was trying to tell me something, yet I didn't know what it was.

From then on, I avoided going to the oak tree, but the image of it kept coming back, even in the evenings when we sat on the porch.

Each evening, I still accurately guessed the cars, so much so that Louie and my grandfather gave up playing. Although, they continued to argue about Fords versus Chevrolets.

During those days, instead of running the dirt path I spent most of my time in my father's old bedroom. My dad was killed in World War II, just at the end. He and his younger brother, my uncle Louie, had been in the same unit in the Marines. My father was eighteen years old when he got killed in 1945.

Louie was one year younger than my father. Louie had just turned seventeen and lied about his age when he joined the Marines. He said the military didn't really care about one's age, for all they needed was living bodies to replace the deal ones.

Uncle Louie made it back from the war, and he moved into the old family home with my grandfather. I joined them when I was five. That's when my mother got re-married and moved to San Diego.

I remember the day she drove me to my grandfather's place, took my hand and pulled me from the car.

She dragged me to the barn where my grandfather and Louie were working, and she said, "I can't take it anymore."

Louie looked up from his workbench and asked, "Take what?"

"This thing," she exclaimed. "He's a handful, and I need to get on with my new life."

She turned around and quickly walked back to her car and drove away.

Uncle Louie looked down at me and said, "Well I'll be."

I didn't know what to think about her driving away but mostly listened to the rumbling sound of her car and the smooth noise as it faded into the distance. It was a light blue 1947 Pontiac.

Louie patted me on the head and said, "Don't worry kid. Me and your grandpa will take care of you."

That was on September 3rd, 1950.

During the following seven years I hadn't seen her again, and I wondered if she would be any good at car-guessing.

CHAPTER 3

My body recovered, but the question of accurately predicting cars stayed in my mind. I still had no clue where that came from, and when I went too deep into this thought, my body trembled. It was a similar reaction to not being able to touch the oak tree. Yet, the question stayed in my mind, like hardened gum stuck under a table, and it needed an answer.

Things were seen like never before. Words flowed like rivers, loud noises were like whirlpools, numbers were colors, and sometimes I saw images behind images.

I repeatedly asked Louie about car-guessing, but it seemed he got tired of me. Once he said, "It's just some weird thing you picked up. Don't worry, the bugs will eventually crawl out of your brain."

At first, I wondered if they would come out of my nose or mouth, or even my ears, but then realized he was trying to be funny. That was not much help. Humor, what makes something funny or not, wasn't easy to understand.

Uncle Louie was always smiling and laughing, but sometimes he concerned me. Most days he worked in our orange orchard with my grandfather, but in the evenings, he drank whiskey. Occasionally in the middle of the night, I heard him stomping around in the backyard yelling crude things about Japs. And he raged about the tragic mistake of Iwo Jima, whatever that was?

My grandfather was different than Uncle Louie. He didn't talk much, and Louie said you could never figure out what he was thinking. My grandfather liked to save things. On one side of our house, there were piles of metal and wood, like rusty washing machines and old broken-down cars from the 1930's and early 40's.

Grandfather didn't throw things away including his daily newspapers. Space was needed for them, so all the furniture was moved out of my father's room, and it became a storage place for papers, from floor to ceiling. We called it the newspaper room.

After the fall from the tree, I spent most of my time in there reading old newspapers. Because of that, my concentration and reading ability improved, and most surprising was my aptitude with numbers.

When I saw numbers, they mixed around me as colorful shapes and swirling rivers. Answers to mathematical questions appeared out of nowhere like the rivers handed them to me.

The newspapers contained a gigantic amount of interesting information, but there were always three things that caught my attention.

The first was an ad that ran every day in the classified section, some days with a picture, but mostly only text. It said, "Think and Grow Rich. Be like Edison and Rockefeller. Buy the book with the time-tested truths written by Napoleon Hill."

When walking in the orange groves, I thought a lot about that ad. People needed to work to earn a living. Or, you need an idea to make money. Uncle Louie often talked about finding a way to make lots of money, and he said, "People need money to live, but having bucket loads of the stuff is even better."

If that was important, what could I do to make money when I

grew up, especially bucket loads of it? Being unsteady on my feet, I couldn't drive a tractor or be a fireman. And for sure, I couldn't do any job that required talking with people. That narrowed my options down to just about nothing.

With car-guessing I won pennies, so that wouldn't help.

But, that ad was fascinating and had possibilities. Surely, I could think and grow rich if someone taught me.

There was a second thing in the newspapers that caught my attention, and it wasn't the funny pages. It was something called the Daily Racing Form.

The third thing was a separate page with lists of short names and numbers. It was titled The New York Stock Exchange. That page was highly confusing, like a mystery needing to be solved.

So, I mainly concentrated on the Daily Racing Form and quickly comprehended that it had to do with horse racing. This page often had a list of horses in the coming races at a place called the Santa Anita Racetrack.

I went through stacks of old newspapers and got to know the names of horses and learned where they finished race after race. In doing this, colorful numbers appeared and flowed forward like competing rivers. Then one of the numbers crossed a line ahead of the others.

Each day after my grandfather got finished with the latest newspaper he handed it to me, and I'd turn to the racing section and look at the results.

Then, one day I realized I had an ability, and connecting that with car-guessing and Napoleon Hill, I got an idea of how that skill might work.

Immediately I went out to the front porch where Louie was sipping from a bottle and asked, "Do you know a place called Santa Anita Racetrack?"

He smiled, "Sure. It's close by. I go there sometimes."

"Can you take me?"

He peered at me and said, "It ain't for kids."

"No, really. Can you take me there?"

"What for?" He asked.

"Because I'd like to see the horses running." Of course, there was more to it. I wanted to see if my ability was real or not.

He took a small sip from the bottle and said, "Okay, why not? Tomorrow we go."

* * *

The racetrack was a busy place. It was February 1958, and the weather was warm. I wore a long-sleeved shirt and a light jacket and tried to look grown-up, but that was impossible for a tall, skinny twelve-year-old boy. In June, I would be thirteen.

We followed what seemed like thousands of people across a massive parking lot, through entrance gates and then under some stands. I put my hand on Louie's shoulder, for the immensity of the crowd made it difficult to concentrate. Crowds made me shuffle when I walked.

Under the stands, we entered a long room, and on one side there were small booths with men in them. People lined up in front of the booths.

I pointed at them and asked, "What are they doing?"

Louie glanced at the booths and then down at me. "Making bets."

"How does it work?"

"It's like when your grandfather and I bet on cars. Only here you choose a horse, and you put some money on the horse. The man over there in the booth gives you a ticket. If the horse wins you bring the ticket back to the booth and he gives you more money than what you bet. It might be double, triple or more depending on the handicap. If you lose, which is most of the time, then you tear up the ticket and throw it on the ground."

When reading the Daily Racing Form in the newspapers, I had already figured out handicaps. From my pocket, I took out a dollar bill that my grandfather gave to me at Christmas.

Louie was looking at the crowd so to get his attention, I waved the Dollar in front of him and said, "I'd like to try it."

He raised an eyebrow. "You're too young."

"You can do it for me."

He was getting jumpy. An announcer said the horses were moving toward the gates and the betting on the first race was ready to close.

Louie gave a nervous grin and said, "I want half your profits if we win."

I anticipated this response and replied. "You also put in a dollar and that way we'll be partners."

"You're kidding," he exclaimed.

"Nope. Let's be partners."

Time was running out. "Okay," he said.

I stuck out my hand and said, "Shake on it."

Louie looked around at the people rushing for the stands, so quickly he reached across and shook my hand. He took his wallet from his back pocket and pulled out a dollar bill. "What horse do we bet on?"

"Alma's Whisper," I said.

"What? The odds are twenty-seven to one on that horse. It doesn't have a chance in hell to win."

"Grandpa says hell isn't a nice word."

Louie rolled his eyes and said, "Okay, sorry kid, but that horse is a loser."

"It will win," I asserted. "It's like the guessing game."

He paused, his eyes wide. "You mean like guessing cars?"

"Yep"

"No way!"

"Yep."

Louie looked at the booths and saw they were ready to close.

He sprinted across the room and gave two dollars to the man in the booth.

* * *

Louie came back to me holding two tickets in his hand and said, "This is beyond crazy. Here I'm putting my fortune into the hands of a twelve-year-old kid that belongs in a lunatic asylum."

By that point, I knew what asylum meant.

We made our way to the stands where we could see the race track. One horse was acting wild and didn't want to go into the starting gate. Six men were trying to push it in. It was Alma's Whisper.

"I can't believe we bet on that nag," Louie blurted out.

Giving no reply, I watched the horses as they waited in the gates and then there was a loud clanging, and the gate doors opened, and the horses shot forward. When they ran past us, I didn't see the horses. It was more like metallic numbers skimming the top of a river. Alma's Whisper was in last place.

"Impossible," Louie moaned.

The horses turned the bend at the far end, and Alma's Whisper began to pass a couple of horses. Then on the far side, it gained on the others. Around the last bend our horse was in third place, and then with long sweeping strides, it began to advance.

At that point, Louie was screaming at the top of his lungs, "Come on, come on, come on!" His fists pumped into the air like pistons in an engine.

Alma's Whisper crossed the line in first place, and Louie jumped up and down while screaming every cuss word in the book. He settled down and said, "I can't believe it kid, but that was wild."

"You are not supposed to cuss like that," I stated.

"Do you realize what just happened?"

"You were cussing. Grandpa says it's not nice."

He raised his eyebrows and took a breath. "Yeah, okay. But that horse could hardly make it to a waterhole let alone win a race. Incredible."

"What happens now?" I asked.

"We go downstairs, collect our fifty-four dollars and go spend it."

"What about the next race?" I asked.

"What do you mean what about it?"

"We should bet the fifty-four dollars on Wind Song."

"Wind-Song? I ain't never heard of that horse."

"Yeah, go collect our money and bet it on Wind-Song in the next race."

"No kidding," he said.

I nodded and said, "Wind-Song." I kept repeating the horse's name for fear he would forget it.

Wind-Song won the next race, and although the odds were less than on Alma's Whisper, we now had a hundred and sixty-two dollars.

Louie wanted to leave the racetrack and spend the money, but I insisted that we stay for the following races. He said that no one was that lucky. I really didn't care about luck, or winning or losing. What was important was to test my ability.

We won all the following races and walked back to Louie's 1940 Ford carrying four brown paper shopping bags filled with nineteen thousand dollars.

Once in the car Louie shook his head and said, "I'll be damned."

I said, "Uncle Louie, you can't use words like that, and whatever happens we can't tell anyone about this."

"It's crazy." His eyes were round like he was lost in a forest.

"Did you hear me?" I asked. "We can't tell anyone about this, not even grandpa."

"Huh... okay."

And that was the beginning of our partnership.

On the way home Louie stopped at a liquor store and bought a bottle of Jack Daniels which cost much more than what he usually drank.

When we got home, he immediately opened the bottle and sipped from it. By the middle of the night, he was in the backyard screaming something about Jap's and Iwo Jima, and I got concerned if he was the right person to have as a partner in my new enterprise. But he was all I had.

CHAPTER 4

We planned to go again to the race track on the following weekend, but it got rained out. Lucky for us the officials rescheduled for February 22nd and March 1st.

I wondered how much we could win and if we would get into trouble if we earned too much. Therefore, based on the first visit I thought we should keep our winnings to less than twenty thousand dollars.

On February 22nd and March 1st, we made a lot of money.

So, after three visits to the race track, we had sixty thousand, four hundred and fourteen dollars and thirty-seven cents. That's after deducting gas for the car, food and the bottles of whiskey and cognac. That's correct. Uncle Louie had now switched from whiskey to cognac.

With the steady supply of cognac, Louie was in seventh heaven. The average yearly salary in the U.S. in 1958 was five thousand, five hundred Dollars. In three visits to Santa Anita, we had made ten times that.

The Santa Anita racing season ended, and we considered what to do next. During our visit to the race track on March 1st Louie met two men who were professional gamblers. Their names were Snodgrass and Minx, and they traveled to race tracks all over the country claiming they made a good living at it.

Louie said we should do the same, suggesting it would be an opportunity to see the world.

When he proposed that, it made me wonder about a couple of things. If we made money at the race tracks, what trouble would Louie get into? And, was I ready to leave our orange grove?

* * *

A reality was sinking in. It actually seemed possible to make money by just thinking, but that created big questions needing answers. Is horse racing what Napoleon Hill meant in his book, Think and Grow Rich? Having not read it, I wasn't sure.

In any case, I needed more practice and how better could I get practice than by seeing the world?

It took some hard negotiating with my grandfather, but he agreed that Louie and I would spend a month or two going around the country. This was on Louie's pretense that, "the kid needs to learn a thing or two about this great land."

We didn't say anything horses and racetracks.

While grandfather reluctantly agreed, I suspected he was glad to get rid of me for a while. He sometimes said he didn't like to travel, preferring to look after the orange trees and work on machinery in the barn. The longest trip he had ever made was when he moved his wife and two young sons from Oklahoma to California. Because of that, we were known as 'Oakies.'

My grandfather also had a sick heart that sped up when it wasn't supposed to. When it happened, he'd lie down, whether in the house, the barn or out in the orange grove.

There was a Mexican named Carlos that lived in a shack on the back of the property, and he worked with the trees and acted as a guard to keep people from stealing our oranges. Louie called him a *wetback*, but I never saw any water on his back other than sweat when he worked. So, with Carlos around, my grandfather had enough help.

On the day we left, I packed some clothing into a cardboard box and walked to Louie's car to put it in the trunk. There, Louie had already placed the dirt-brown suitcase where we kept all our winnings.

"We can't take all that money," I exclaimed.

"What do you mean? We might need it," he argued.

"What if it gets stolen?"

"Naw. Who's going to steal something out of a 1940 Ford?"

"We don't need sixty thousand dollars for this trip."

"Sure, we do. We want to have fun."

I knew what he meant. If Louie had his way, he'd spend it all on whiskey and chasing girlfriends. "I'm not going," I said, removing my box of clothing from the car and walking back toward the house.

"No, wait," Louie cried out.

I turned back, looked at him and said, "Let's take one thousand dollars and leave the rest."

He frowned, and it seemed he was doing serious thinking. "Okay," he agreed. "So, what should we do with this suitcase of money?"

"Let's stop at the bank on our way out of town," It was probably safer to put the money in a bank than leave it under a bed, but red flashes exploded in my mind. There were pros and cons to giving Uncle Louie access to a bank account with so much money, mostly cons.

* * *

Our goal was to cross the country and go to Louisville, Kentucky where there was a racetrack called Churchill Downs. Once a year the best horses in America went there for a famous race called the Kentucky Derby. It took us three weeks to get there. Louie's 1940 Ford broke down two times along the way, and we spent a lot to get it fixed.

When we arrived in Louisville, all the hotels were full because of the Derby. So, Louie and I slept in the car. It was just as well. We only had twenty-five dollars left because of expensive car repairs. Replacing an engine wasn't cheap, and Louie said the mechanics had overcharged for their work.

I suspected Louie was also spending money on things I didn't know about.

We found a campground that cost twenty-five cents a night, and I was glad it had showers and latrines, as Louie called them. Louie slept on the front seat of the car, and I slept on the back seat.

In the evening, we cooked hotdogs over an open fire, and Louie grumbled, and I guessed he was having that emotion called anger.

"Damn it," he said. "We should have brought that money."

"Grandpa said not to use cuss words," I stated.

"I'll use any word I want," he countered.

I knew he was tired from the driving and all the stress from the breakdowns, but I suspected there was something else. "We'll do okay," I claimed.

"I'm banking my entire life on some hair-brained trip and a kid with the intelligence of an egg. Santa Anita was blind luck, and now I'm halfway around the world sitting on my haunches breathing smoke from a fire and eating burnt hot dogs."

He made it sound like burnt hot dogs was a bad thing.

To know if any food was good or bad wasn't easy for me because each food gave a different sensation. For instance, when I ate a red chili pepper that Carlos gave me, I had an orange electrical sensation. Other foods gave me different impressions. Rather than complicating things for Louie, I stated, "The hot dogs are juicy with crusty edges."

"Kid, you drive me nuts," he said. "This trip has been crazy."

"Well, at least we got to see the country."

"Yeah, and how are we gonna get home? We won't make it on twenty-five bucks."

As he talked, the brilliant colors of the campfire invaded my senses, and I thought of the races we'd see at Churchill Downs. From reading the Daily Racing Form, I knew all the horses in each race, their numbers now mixing with the flames of the fire. It was like our oak tree had become giant red and was towering over our heads.

"The races will be interesting," I said, switching my thoughts to the horses and seeing the vibrant metallic colored rivers battling each other to a finish line.

"This is insane," he muttered. "We are in the land of famous whiskey, and I need some."

He stomped off in the direction of some buildings just beyond the campground where there was a liquor store.

Then it became clear what really bothered him and that concerned me more than anything. In the newspapers, I had read about something called alcoholics, and in watching Louie, I realized that he craved alcohol. It was known as an addiction, and that created erratic behavior and other problems.

I needed to prepare for this for I saw dark days ahead. Since my fall from the oak tree, I was becoming increasingly aware of the direction of events, especially if I had some history to build on. If there was historical momentum, the rivers made accurate predictions of what was going to happen.

With Louie, I had enough history to see hurt coming.

* * *

The following morning, I woke up in the back seat of our car. Uncle Louie wasn't in the front seat. Conflicting colors filled the vehicle, shades of carrot orange, magenta, and fluorescent green.

Did he take a bus back to California? When he walked away the previous evening, he was cussing and was in that state where he did irregular things. Sometimes he did this at the farm, disappearing for days at a time. I wondered if he abandoned me. If yes, then I needed a plan.

I got dressed and headed toward the latrine and saw Louie stretched out across a bench. When I got up to him, he smelled of stale alcohol and vomit. A near empty bottle of Kentucky Bourbon was on the ground. I picked it up and poured the last remaining portion onto the brown earth and then put the empty bottle in a trash can.

After I slapped him a few times on the face, he began to stir.

"Huh. Whazz-at," he slurred.

"Louie, you've got to wake up."

With blurred eyes, he asked, "Where's my bottle?"

"Finished. You don't need it."

He looked at me with mean eyes. "Like heck, I don't. You don't know what I need."

"Give it a break," I told him. "We've got to get to the racetrack."

He looked around the campground and said, "Okay. I guess we should go."

He sat up and for a while held his head in his hands, and then he stood up, and we walked over to the building with the showers. We both stripped down and washed. The water was cold, so I didn't stay long, but Louie was still standing under the running water even after I dressed. I went back to the car and waited.

Eventually, he came to the car looking better. Then, he changed into a clean shirt and pants, and we headed for Churchill Downs.

It was an immense place with thousands of people. Flashes of brilliant colors were going off like fireworks, more than I could handle, so I squinted my eyes and focused on the ground.

I put my hand on Louie's shoulder and shuffled my feet, concentrating on the asphalt, noticing the subtle details of black and dark blues, and oily film that had hardened and worn smooth over time.

It took a while, but I finally glanced up and saw that most of the men wore suits and fedora hats, and the women wore elegant dresses. It was like pictures I'd seen of people going to church, almost like the Kentucky Derby was a religious day.

A man in a uniform came up to us and said, "Children are not allowed here."

Louie tapped his head with his finger and told the man, "The kid ain't all there. He needs to stick with me at all times."

The man looked down at me, nodded and walked away. I saw other kids in the crowd, so it seemed the rule wasn't strictly applied.

Like we had done at Santa Anita, I chose the horses and Louie placed the bets. We put ten dollars on the first race and our horse lost.

The moment the horses crossed the finish line Louie threw up his hands and said, "This is the most absurd thing I've ever done in my life to trust a twelve-year-old simpleton," the words flowing from his mouth like long strings of swirling red spaghetti.

I stared into the distance, wondering why my guess was wrong. There didn't seem to be an answer. Maybe it was the crowd and the emotions in the air that threw me off. I backtracked up a river in my head and realized my calculations were wrong. At the campfire, when looking at the red flaming oak tree, a six had mistakenly been reversed for a nine, and that meant betting on the wrong horse. More attention to detail was needed.

Two men walked over and said, "Hello Louie. You're a long way from California."

It was Snodgrass and Minx, the two professional gamblers we had met at Santa Anita.

Louie's face turned from anger to resignation. "I didn't expect to see you two again," he said.

Minx said, "We go to all the big races, especially the Triple Crown. Who are you betting on today?"

"For what?" Louie asked.

"The Kentucky Derby. The big one."

"Not a clue in the world," Louie responded. "I'm down to my last ten bucks."

Snodgrass raised his eyebrows and said, "That's tough." He looked at me, then back at Louie and remarked, "Seems you still have the little dimwit with you. His big round blue eyes look like portholes into nothingness." Snodgrass laughed.

My hand rested on Louie's shoulder for support.

Louie nodded. "Yeah, I've got to take care of him."

A teacher once commented that I reacted to things differently than other kids. For instance, you are supposed to get angry if people called you names like a dimwit or an idiot. Instead, when Snodgrass said it, I saw dark gray, like the clouds in parts of Kansas. I said, "Tim Tam will win the derby today."

The two men looked at me and laughed. "Impossible," Snodgrass said. "That's a good horse, but it only came in fifth in its last race. We'll take Silky Sullivan. Bill Shoemaker is the jockey, and he doesn't lose."

"You're wrong," I said, knowing that Silky Sullivan was the favorite, but favorites don't always win.

Minx laughed. "It looks like you'll be hitchhiking back to the West Coast. We'll see you Louie, and good luck with the little moron."

They turned and walked away. From reading the newspaper, I knew what moron meant. I pondered why this man would call me that. And, how was I supposed to react?

For the second race, Louie reluctantly accepted my guess and placed ten dollars on it. Our horse won with twelve to one odds.

We won in the following races, always keeping enough money in reserve to get back to California. The last race of the day was the Kentucky Derby, and the odds were three to one for Tim Tam. We placed ten thousand dollars on the horse.

When the race began, it was different than the races at Santa Anita Racetrack where people were noisy. Before the Kentucky Derby race, the crowd went quiet, and it was like silent silver-gray impulses hovered over the stands.

When the race started, the impulses exploded, and a powerful deep vibration moved through the crowd. A thunderous cloud enveloped the race track, and I watched it turn into molten dark purple sweeping around the track. The significance of it was hard to interpret and seemed like a cloud of emotion. I didn't know if it was the emotion of hope or greed, or even of fear. From my hours of reading the dictionary, I understood how these emotions were defined, but I had never directly experienced them. Now I perceived them in the crowd of people.

For a moment, I lost attention when thinking about emotions, but then the horses ran past us, and I only saw metallic images. When they got to the backstretch, Tim Tam was just behind the leader Lincoln Road. Silky Sullivan ridden by Bill Shoemaker was lagging the field.

At the turn, Tim Tam made a move, and in the final stretch, the horse passed Lincoln Road, and Tim Tam won by half a length as Louie's strong fingers squeezed my forearm.

The vibrations of the crowd settled down, and I heard people around us exclaiming surprise about Bill Shoemaker and Silky Sullivan. Images flowed from their mouths and filled the sky like oddly shaped balloons. Then the balloons popped and vanished like dissipating hopes.

We went to the betting booths and collected our money. Louie didn't say a word but only shook his head, and it was unusual to see him speechless.

Churchill Downs had a place where you could send winnings to your bank, so we sent twenty-five thousand dollars to our bank in California and kept five thousand to pay for travel expenses.

We walked back to the car and Louie became ecstatic, like waking from a stupor. "This is incredible," he said. "We are so, da... ah... darned lucky."

I knew he wanted to use a cuss word, for that's how he spoke much of the time, yet I sensed he was suddenly respectful because of what had just happened. "We can't tell anyone," I reminded him.

"No one would believe it," he exclaimed.

"Even so, I beg you to keep your mouth shut."

He wasn't listening. Instead, he laughed and said, "They should change the name of this town to Louie's Ville.

It was May 3rd, 1958 and soon I would be thirteen years old in June.

CHAPTER 5

We had achieved our goal of going to the Kentucky Derby, and now we faced the long trip back to California. The thought of our orange grove triggered soft sweet smells of orange blossoms that tugged at me like a magnet.

After getting in the car, Louie said, "Let's go to Baltimore."

"What for?" I asked.

"The Preakness. The second leg of the Triple Crown."

The vibration of the crowd was still fresh in my mind, and it made me dizzy and disoriented. "I don't want to," I said.

"Come on kid, we're on a roll. Let's have a little fun."

I didn't need fun. In fact, fun is an emotion, and I'm not sure what it is. But then a thought went through my head. It had to do with Napoleon Hill. What better place could I think and grow rich than at the Preakness in Baltimore?

"Okay, let's go," I said.

* * *

We drove from Louisville to Baltimore stopping at a minor race track along the way. Our betting there wasn't big, not wanting to "break the bank," as Louie said. Even so, we stopped at a Ford dealership and used the winnings to trade in the 1940 Ford for a brand-new Ford Fairlane 500 Convertible. With Louie, it had to be a Ford. The salesman was amazed when we paid with cash from a brown paper bag, for I saw yellow flashes emanate from his head when Louie opened the bag.

Louie said that the Ford Fairlane 500 Convertible was the best car in America and would be ideal back in California for attracting the ladies.

We also stopped at a store and bought new clothing, jeans and white t-shirts for me. Louie said that was, "the cat's pajamas," because that's how James Dean and Elvis Presley dressed. Louie bought a new suit and a fedora hat, "to blend in with others at the racetracks."

* * *

The Pimlico Race Course was in Baltimore where they held the Preakness Stakes, the second race in the Triple Crown.

On the day of the race we again ran into Snodgrass and Minx, the two professional gamblers and when Minx saw us, he whistled and said, "The simpleton made a right call back in Louisville with Tim Tam. Looks like you got new duds?"

A lot of people called clothing 'duds.' Like so many expressions, the logic was not evident. How do you connect cloth with a dud, whatever that was?

"Who are you betting on today on the Preakness," Snodgrass asked.

"Tim Tam," I said.

"That's not going to happen," Snodgrass countered. "The probabilities are very low. It's got to be Silky Sullivan.

I realized that Snodgrass and Minx were locked into believing in Silky Sullivan and no convincing would change their minds. I had seen that with people. For instance, Louie was locked into Fords and my grandfather with Chevrolets. I guessed that's how it is with people. They put their faith into something, and no logic or reason could change them.

I looked at Snodgrass and said, "Think about what you believe. It could be wrong."

He laughed at me, and I wondered why?

That afternoon Tim Tam won the second leg of the Triple Crown, and we sent another thirty thousand dollars back to California.

From there we went to the Belmont Park in Elmont, New York where the last Triple Crown race took place, the Belmont

Stakes.

By then Louie was all smiles, making jokes and singing the songs of Frank Sinatra. I told him to bet our money on a horse named Cavan, and he resisted. Tim Tam had won the Kentucky Derby and the Preakness so it would be historic if it won the Triple Crown, and all Louie's hopes were on that. We argued for a long time, and finally, he placed a bed on Cavan.

Tim Tam led through most of the race and Louie was in agony, but in the home stretch Cavan took the lead and won by two lengths.

We sent forty thousand back to our bank in California and kept a little over ten thousand with us.

It was June 7th, 1958.

* * *

On the way to the car, Louie walked just in front of me, and I held his shoulder. I turned and noticed two men quickly walking behind us. That gave me a flash of lightning and a dark mauve image, and then things happened too fast to react when one of the men came up behind me and grabbed me, and with difficulty, he lifted me off the ground because I was taller than him. He was incredibly powerful and squeezed my chest so I could barely breathe. I tried to kick back into him, but it was like trying to kick a telephone pole.

The other man had a small wooden club and quickly moved toward Louie. I cried out, but it was too late. As Louie turned, the man raised the club, and with a swift movement he blindsided Louie on the head, and a second later, like a rag doll, Louie crumbled to the ground. The man with the wooden club picked up the paper bag with our money, and the other man released me. They ran through the parking lot.

I shuffled three steps to a car and put my hand on its fender to keep from wobbling, as violet purple images transformed to flashes of red and electric yellow. Louie groaned, rolled to his side and sat up. He rubbed the side of his head and murmured, "Memories of damn Iwo Jima."

In the distance, I saw the robbers run past Snodgrass and Minx who grinned and waved at the men.

Once Louie regained his senses I said, "We should tell the police."

He looked at me with resigned eyes. "Are you kidding me? Who would believe us? We need to cut and run."

He was right. We had no proof that anything had been stolen.

Ten thousand dollars had been taken from us, but Louie still had our "going home" money in one of his pockets, so we went to our car and began the long drive back to California taking Route 66 after we got to Chicago.

In Litchfield, Illinois we stayed at the Belvidere Motel. In the motel café, I ate fried chicken which hit my taste buds with soft brown colors, and then I went to bed.

It was June 12th, 1958 and it was my birthday, and I turned thirteen years old. Louie stayed up late because there was a dance floor in the café and he wanted to meet girlfriends.

* * *

We continued along Route 66 through Oklahoma. Louie said he didn't have many memories of living there as a kid, although people called us Oakies because that's where we originated from.

Most of the way back to California we rode in silence with the top down and Louie seemed to enjoy our new car. Not talking gave me time to think and during parts of the trip I laid down in the back seat and watched the changing contours of the distant horizon.

The scenery along Route 66 was remarkable with farms and

ranches and mountains and vast desert expanses that stretched the length of the world.

My thoughts went back to Belmont Park and the purple colors I had seen when those men approached us. What they did wasn't right, but there was a more in-depth consideration. What was it that decided if something was right or wrong? I wasn't sure how we come to that conclusion unless a person tells you what is right or wrong. It's like my grandfather saying that cussing is wrong.

But then again, who told my grandfather what is right and wrong and how did that person come to that conclusion? Even more confusing, what happens when one person says something is right, but another says that same something is wrong? So, who is right and who is wrong, and is there an ultimate decision maker?

What happened in that parking lot at Belmont Park made me realize something about people, that there is something in them that can make you jumpy and wobbly. When having that thought, I noticed storm clouds on the horizon and they swirled and warned me to be cautious around people, and of course, to look out for men with clubs.

The looks on the faces of Snodgrass and Minx stayed with me, and I connected them with the men who had robbed us. The clouds were telling me to recognize people like that and to be careful around them.

The clouds communicated something else. A better understanding of life was needed, in order to achieve my goal to think and grow rich. There was much to learn.

Definitely, I could weave together the history on The Daily Racing Form, but the crowds of people at the races unsettled me, and men like Snodgrass and Minx made it even worse.

Was it possible that there were other ways to think and become rich? When I thought about it, I didn't really know why getting rich was so important. I guess there were other things to do in life, but I wasn't sure what they were. I still didn't think I would make a good teacher or policeman or fireman. Because of who I was, I wasn't sure I could perform accurately in any kind of full-time job.

At the same time, I knew I could achieve specific goals, like running to the oak tree at the edge of the orange farm, and doing it repeatedly, or like reading the newspaper at a particular time every day and forecasting the outcomes of horse races.

But, after that event in Belmont Park, the thought of horse racing created greenish yellow vomit colors, especially when I thought of Snodgrass and Minx. Was there a different way to think and grow rich?

CHAPTER 6

When we got back to our farm, my grandfather held a delayed birthday party for me. He was angry that we had been gone so long. And, he was angry that we showed up in a new red convertible, and he was especially mad that it was a Ford and not a Chevrolet.

On the picnic table in the backyard. Carlos joined us, and for the first time in my life, I had a real birthday cake rather than a cupcake with a candle in it. Louie had bought the cake at a shop in town.

My grandfather gave me an envelope with a birthday card in it, the card decorated with vibrant red and blue and yellow balloons, and a cartooney clown. In the card was a dollar bill.

Holding the dollar gave me images of green corn fields like we had seen in Illinois, stretching endlessly for miles.

Louie got his Brownie camera and took a picture of my grandfather and me sitting in front of the cake while I was holding the dollar. Louie winked and said, "Bet you ain't seen one of those before."

After that, when we were alone and away from grandfather, Louie kept talking about going to Santa Anita when it opened for the winter season, but I was against it. I didn't want to see him get clubbed again, or even something worse.

So, we settled back into our regular routine with Louie working with my grandfather and Carlos in the orchard, and me puttering around the house. Sometimes I ran the path to the end of the farm, but that routine didn't have the same effect as in the past, and I was still unable to touch the oak tree.

In the evenings, we didn't spend as much time on the front porch, because Louie was usually gone. Often, I heard him come home late at night with a slam of the car door and feet stumbling toward the house. More than once I listened to my grandfather cursing at Louie that he had to stop going to the nightclubs and gambling dens.

We had over a hundred and forty-one thousand dollars in our bank account when I added up all the winnings we made. Of course, Louie had access to that money, and I didn't know how much he was spending. And, that concerned me.

When my mother went off with her new husband, she opened a bank account in my name and deposited three dollars in it. She told my grandfather she would keep putting money in the account to help pay for my care. She never did. The balance stayed at three dollars plus some interest. At least the account existed, and I thought I might be able to use it if I ran into problems with Louie.

Sometimes I thought about my mother and her life. At seventeen years old, she was already a widow when I was born. Her husband, my father, was killed in the Pacific in March of 1945. They met in 1944 after he finished boot camp, just before they shipped him off to the Pacific. Louie told me that my father saw her walking through a park, and a day later they ran off to Las Vegas and got married. He was eighteen, and she was sixteen.

I was born nine months after that on June 12th,, 1945, several months after his death. Louie said that she claimed I was an awkward baby, never crying but always whimpering non-stop, night and day. My first words were spoken when I was four years old.

So, the logic all made sense, that my mother should have a new and different life. I didn't know anything about her like what she was doing and exactly where she lived. Maybe she even had some children. Someday it might be interesting to find out what happened to her. But those thoughts were secondary as I mostly concentrated on daily routines.

Once when my grandfather was finished with the daily paper, I opened it to a page and asked him, "What are all those numbers?"

"That's the stock prices," he said.

"What are stock prices?"

He shook his head and said, "I'm not sure. It has to do with buying and selling shares in companies. I've never done it, so don't know much about it. In 1929 people lost fortunes in the stock market and we went into the Great Depression. In Oklahoma, it got terrible, and eventually, I had to sell our farm. A lot of Oakie's like us moved to California. I wouldn't touch the stock market."

"How can we find out more?" I asked.

"Maybe someone at the bank would know, but it ain't worth it."

I thought about that and said, "Let's wait. I'd like to spend some time looking at these numbers to see what they tell me."

"Tell you?" He asked.

"Something like that," I replied.

"You're one strange kid," he commented.

I stared at him wishing I knew how other kids would respond to what he said. That was something I needed to learn, to become wise in the ways of the world. Maybe by carefully observing the reactions of other people I could practice their responses, so it would look like I was normal in showing emotions.

But, I knew that my true way was different than others. If you asked me if I was happy or sad, I'm not sure I could tell you, as most of the time I experienced things in colors, clouds, bubbles, rivers, and numbers.

With the latest newspaper in my hand, I went back into my father's old bedroom. The big question was what those numbers meant and if I could use them, as I had done with horse racing?

I figured that with horse racing my mind was using past numbers to work out some kind of probability. Actually, it was more like a certainty than a probability. Louie said I was an equestrian prophet, but that term didn't mean much to me.

With horse racing, each horse and the number assigned to it was associated with a color in my head. Past results became colorful rivers extending into the future. Would that work with these stock price numbers?

I looked at the numbers, and they didn't make sense. The title at the top of the page said, Today's Quotations, and underneath were headers saying Sales in Hundreds and High, Low, Close and Chg. Under the headers were columns where there were short names like Abbott L and Penny J.C., followed by sets of numbers like 24 ½ and 9 ¾. Eventually, I figured out those numbers meant 24.50 and 9.75.

Once I had some history, the numbers took on significance, and I saw something like direction, also mixed in with force or momentum. I learned that those short names were companies and in my mind, each company had a different colored cloud, either expanding or contracting. Many of the clouds influenced each other, so one had to look at the entirety as well as the individual parts. Once I had a few days of history, the cloud became a river. Then, the rivers extend into the future where some took on bright tones, and others became shades of dark purple and blue.

It was much more complicated than horse racing, and it took time to see patterns. Then, I began to make accurate predictions but didn't know how they might be applied.

I went to Louie and showed him the page with the New York Stock Exchange numbers and said, "Can we go to the bank to find out about this?"

"About what?"

"Grandpa said the bank can tell us more about stocks and stuff like that. How it works, like buying and selling them."

Louie paused, and his eyes became wide. "You mean you're getting premonitions about this?"

"What are premonitions?" I asked.

"Omens, like with the horses, which one will win."

"Well, not exactly, but maybe something like that."

Louie was silent and stood frozen for a moment and then grinned, and said, "Well, I'll be damned. For sure, we'll go tomorrow."

CHAPTER 7

We lived in a small town known in California as an *orange-grove* town, so our bank didn't deal much with stocks in companies. Our bank manager arranged a meeting with someone at a big headquarter bank in downtown Los Angeles. I was amazed how he kept saying, "Mister Harkin" to Uncle Louie.

Whenever our local bank manager glanced at me, he quickly turned back to Louie.

Before we left the bank, we received a statement of our bank account. It was now slightly above one hundred and nineteen thousand dollars. In just a few weeks it had dropped over twenty-one thousand.

That was a lot of missing money, and it confirmed there was a problem that needed fixing, but I wasn't sure what to do.

When we got into the car, I looked at Louie and asked, "What happened to our money?

He turned away from me and looked across the street at two young women who were staring at our bright red convertible Ford. They wore cotton dresses and bright red lipstick, and they had a similar hairstyle as Marilyn Monroe who had been on the cover of Life Magazine.

Louie smiled at them and then turned to me and asked, "What did you say?"

"Our money. A lot is gone."

"What do you mean?"

"Our account is down over twenty-one thousand dollars."

"Oh yeah. There were some expenses."

"Like what?"

"Ah... New ventures and public relations. I expanded out from horses and bet on baseball games."

"And did it work?" I asked.

He hesitated and glanced back at the two women. "Well, it worked some of the time."

"But not always," I stated.

"Okay, I lost some, but there's plenty left."

"And what are those public relations?"

"I had to interview some, ah, ladies, thinking we might need a secretary, and there were expenses for dinners and drinks and whatnot."

I'd learned that an ordinary person would feel anger over

this, but I was sensing a rainbow that started out with regular rainbow colors that then arced downwards and blended into something dark.

Louie's spending habits didn't make any sense. After our trip to the East Coast I realized that you needed money to make money, so why carelessly spend it?

"I thought we were partners," I stated.

"We are, kid. It's just that I need some discretionary money."

I thought about it and quickly came up with a solution. "Okay. We are equal partners so here's the deal. Every time you take a dollar from the account, I will withdraw a dollar, one for one."

He peered at me like he didn't know where I was going and said, "I don't understand."

"It's easy arithmetic. If you spend a hundred dollars from our account, then I will take out one hundred. That's a fair partnership."

His eyes tightened up, and he took a breath and said, "I guess it makes sense."

"Then I'll take twenty-one thousand from our partnership pot. And, from now on you can spend whatever you want from our shared pot, as long as I always take an equal amount."

"Ah... Darn. I ain't sure where this is headed," he said.

"That's the deal," I stated. "Otherwise we don't go see the banker in L.A."

Louie sneered at me, and I could see he didn't like this arrangement. He ran his fingers through his hair and said, "Okay, I agree, I guess."

We returned to the bank and transferred over twenty thousand dollars into my three-dollar personal account.

Back in the car Louie started it and drove away from the curb. The two women were still standing on the other side of the street. They looked in our direction with smiles on their faces. Louie had a sour, stern look and stared straight ahead into the traffic.

In the middle of the street, I saw a massive cloudy black fist, maybe more like a catcher's mitt pounding the ground. Our car was headed toward the mitt, and I perceived the car being crushed. It told me the agreement with Louie was not a long-term solution, for as long as he was running around at night, there would be problems.

CHAPTER 8

We arrived at the headquarters bank in Los Angeles. The men working there were dressed in suits with white shirts and dark ties. Women wore bright cotton dresses. Louie and I were in short-sleeved shirts, jeans, and sneakers. Louie muttered, "I shoulda worn my suit."

After we told a reception lady who we were, she led us to a desk where she asked us to sit in two chairs. There was no one behind the desk, and it didn't have anything on it other than a pad of blank paper and a nameplate that said, "Grant Adams – Senior Manager – Investments." We waited for a few minutes, and a man joined us.

Louie stood up, so I did too. The man stuck out his hand, and Louie shook it.

Then the man said, "I'm Grant Adams.

He patted me on my left shoulder, and his hand felt like a sponge, not like the firm hands of my grandfather and Louie, and Carlos.

"Please take your seats." He said, "How may I help you?"

Our seats were wooden whereas his chair was covered in brown leather.

Louie replied, "We got some money to invest like in the stock market and that sort of thing."

"We?" Grant Adams asked.

"Yeah, me and my nephew, Arlo." Red sparkles went off in my head, for Louie rarely said my name, usually just calling me kid.

Adams looked at me with a still face, eyebrows down forcing two wrinkle lines on his forehead. He said, "Oh, yes, of course."

"We want to know how it works," Louie stated.

"It's actually quite simple," Adams said. "First you put your funds into a portfolio account, and we administer the trade according to your instruction, whenever you want to buy or sell shares in companies." He paused and asked, "Have you ever done this before?"

"Naw, but we got good for investing in things?" Louie claimed.

"Really?" Adams asked.

"Yeah, we won at the horse races and now want to try other investment stuff."

Adams lowered his eyebrows again, the wrinkles like little canyons. "I see. Well, I'd advise you to consider something. Do you want to make the investment decisions yourselves, or have someone from our bank manage the account on your behalf?"

Louie looked at me and then at Grant Adams. "We don't want nobody else makin' choices. We pick our own horses." He looked again at me and grinned like he was happy he made a joke.

"There are risks with that alternative," Adams said.

"Yeah, yeah, we know about risks," Louie said. "Doing the pickin' is no problem for us."

"Okay, that's your decision, and we are here to support you. Do you know what you want to invest in?"

I interjected, "There are two accounts to invest. With the largest one, we want to put fifty thousand dollars on Penny J.C."

"You mean J.C. Penny?"

"No, Penny J.C., like on the New York Stock Exchange quotes in the newspaper," I replied.

"Oh, yes, I see. Okay, although putting so much money on one stock represents a considerable risk. It's not recommended to put all your eggs in one basket."

I shook my head. "Put it all on Penny J.C."

Adams got some papers to be signed, and we opened two portfolio accounts, one linked to our partnership account. The other was connected to my savings account, the one my mother opened for me in my name. Then on a special banking form, he wrote the details of the trade for Penny J.C. and Louie signed it. "Is there anything else?" He asked.

"Yes, I replied. From the second account, take twenty thousand dollars and put it on corn futures."

Grant Adams eyebrows rose. "What do you know about corn futures?"

"Twenty thousand on corn futures," I said.

Adams took out a form, wrote the details and handed it to Louie. I reached over, slid it away from him and said, "It's my account."

Adams said, "This is highly unusual. You need an adult to countersign this order."

"My name is on the account," I stated, knowing that my mother also had a signature on the account, as well as my grandfather. I signed the form and handed it to Adams.

His smile looked stiff, and he said, "I'll execute the orders immediately."

He left his desk and walked out of the room. It took fifteen minutes, and when he came back, he confirmed that the trade orders were made. We talked some more, like what grandfather called 'chit-chat.' Then Grant Adams walked with us to the front door of the bank. This time he shook my hand rather than patting me on the shoulder.

As we drove away in our bright red Ford convertible, Adams stood on the sidewalk in front of the bank and stared at us, the furrows on his forehead like deep magenta and orange canyons.

CHAPTER 9

The worried look on Grant Adam's face meant that something bothered him. It was impossible to know, except he warned us about risk-taking.

He might be right, for what did I really know about stocks and futures? The magenta and orange colors churned around me. Did I know enough about these things to be investing thousands of dollars? Maybe I should have started with smaller amounts

Before we went to the bank in Los Angeles, I had read about futures as they were featured in a Sunday edition of the Los Angeles Examiner. I learned a lot from reading newspapers, and the Sunday edition had interesting articles about people in Hollywood, politics, art and culture, religion, investing and want-ads.

One article in the Business Section was on futures, and it said this form of trading had been around for a long time. There was a philosopher in Greece, and he mentioned futures in one of his writings, but he didn't call it futures.

Futures were different than bonds and stocks, where you either made loans to companies or bought shares in companies. Futures were a way to make an agreement to buy or sell stocks at some point in time at a fixed price.

The article in the newspaper said that futures were precariously risky and I had to read the article several times before eventually figuring out how futures work. Besides stocks, you could also do futures with something called commodities, which was nothing more than oil, and wheat and stuff like that.

With the instructions I gave in the bank, all my money was now dependent on the price of corn. That investment decision was made because of a golden cloud that formed a river which I had seen when reading the corn commodities prices in the newspaper.

Indeed, perhaps Grant Adams was right. It wasn't a good thing to put all my money on futures for I might lose everything. At the same time, I was okay with it, for it was most important to find out if my ability applied to other things than just guessing cars and horses.

After visiting the bank, Louie and I looked at the stock page of the newspaper every day. Penny J.C. had gone up over ten percent which meant our account had increased by five thousand dollars.

Louie was upset with this because it was much less than what we got at the race track. Yet, that was almost as much as the average person made in a year.

What was of interest to me was to see the way the corn price shot up, just as I had seen in the golden river. The twenty thousand dollars in my personal account had grown to over fifty thousand.

From the stock page in the newspaper, I saw that momentums were weakening, so I spoke with Louie, and he called Mr. Adams, and we sold the holdings in both accounts. Then we made another investment. In our partnership account, we bought Universal Pictures at 19 5/8 and from my personal account, I invested in oats futures.

As Louie set the telephone down, I heard a loud knocking on the back door. It opened, and Carlos stuck his head inside, and he cried out, "Senior Louie. You must come, *pronto*. There is something wrong with Senior Harkin."

Louie charged out the back door, and I followed, and we ran into the middle of the orange grove. My grandfather was lying on his back under the shade of an orange tree. He wasn't moving.

"What happened," Louie asked.

"He does like this." Carlos bent forward and put his hands on his chest. "Then he made sounds like, ugh, ugh, ugh. And then he went on the ground, and I run to you."

Louie leaned down and put his fingers on grandpa's wrist. Then a moan came from somewhere deep inside Louie. "Ahhhhhhhh" The word was a long gray stream that flowed from his mouth, penetrating the orange trees around us. Then he yelled out, "Damn Iwo Jima." Tears ran down his cheeks as he went to his knees and took my grandfather's hand and Louie held it between his two hands, like protecting a hurt sparrow.

When I looked at my grandfather, he seemed quiet and peaceful like a burden had been lifted from him. In the Sunday religious section of the newspaper, I had read an interview of a reverend who spoke about the eternity of the soul and this place of rest which he called heaven.

The article had a lot of logic to it, and now I pictured my grandfather in a place with translucent colors. Louie's moans somehow confirmed this, for they mixed with a gray translucent cloud hovering above us that dissipated into the powder blue air.

The funeral ceremony was at the small Baptist church in town, and all the local farmers were there, and it seemed like a lot of people liked my grandfather. I wore a white dress shirt with a black tie, dark pants and tennis shoes. Louie wore his suit.

The minister spoke about a song that said this world was not our home, but we are just a-passing through and how our treasures were laid out somewhere beyond the blue. Then he gave this quote about God's love.

I couldn't follow everything he said because of the stained-glass windows at the front of the church, and the blue and red clouds flowing from them were a distraction.

Louie had told me this would be an open casket funeral and he asked if it was okay with me.

Indeed, my grandfather was lying in a white painted box at the front of the room. Inside the box was pearl colored cloth that seemed smooth and soft, like he was comfortable and sleeping, only he didn't move.

I wondered if I could stay that still for that long of a time.

They closed the box, and then six of our farmer neighbors lifted it by the brass handles attached on the sides. They carried it outside and placed the box in a long black Cadillac station wagon. My grandfather would like that because Cadillacs were made by the same company that made Chevrolets. We followed it in our red Ford all the way to the cemetery. Grandfather didn't like Fords.

Grandpa was buried next to my grandmother.

CHAPTER 10

Louie didn't talk much during the days after the funeral, but he drank a lot. His eyes were always red.

Every day I walked from the house to the oak tree at the far edge of the property and stood and sometimes thought about my grandfather, but mostly considered Napoleon Hill. It was not so much his book, which I still hadn't read, but more about the fundamental concept to think and grow rich.

The word 'grow' spun around me, and I stood for hours in front of the tree thinking about it. Here was this sizeable sturdy tree that one day was a little acorn. Now it grew so big and powerful that it discharged flashing yellow electricity and it couldn't be touched. Is that what would happen when you grow rich?

Seven days after the funeral I spoke with Mr. Adams on the telephone. Louie had disappeared for two days which he had also done in the past. I sold our positions in Universal Studios and oats futures, and our accounts were in cash.

After that, the stock market was in turmoil, and I couldn't keep up with the movements. Anyway, my thoughts were in other places as I kept seeing my grandfather sitting next to a sparkling silver river, so bright that it hurt your eyes.

Louie came back but disappeared again, and the house was quiet. Sometimes I'd walk to the back of the orchard to talk with Carlos. He had worked for my grandfather for three years and knew everything about managing orange trees. Carlos had family in Mexico and went there every couple of months, but now he made a point to stick around because my grandfather was gone.

"He was a good man," Carlos said.

"I know," I replied, still confused on what good was and how to tell what was good or not.

Without Louie and my grandfather there, something was different, and the oak tree expressed that difference. It was now radiating a dark brown that quickly faded and vanished like it didn't have a direction and was lost.

After talking with Carlos, I went back to the house and heard the telephone ring, and I answered it. "Hello, this is Arlo Harkin."

"Hello Arlo, is your uncle there? This is Grant Adams."

"He's not here," I said. "What is it?"

"Ah, I'm not sure you know about it, but there was a withdrawal from your account."

"Our partnership account?"

"No. From your personal account."

"Did Louie take the money?" I asked.

"No. Your uncle doesn't have a signature on your account. It was your mother."

"My mother?" I hadn't heard anything from her in seven years. "How much did she take?"

"She nearly emptied your account, seventy-five thousand dollars. There are a thousand dollars left in it."

From what he said, I expected to see ominous dark gray

clouds that people might associate with the word 'bad.' Instead, I saw a gray river splitting into its base colors of white and black. I followed the black river, and eventually, it crashed over a never-ending waterfall. That led me to logic. It would be a waste of time to try and chase the money.

Therefore, I backtracked to the white river and followed it a while, and the logic from it told me that I needed to be better at protecting my holdings. Otherwise, I could never be able to think and grow rich.

The people that took my money appeared as flocks of buzzards picking away at a dead animal until nothing was left. What were the reasons these buzzards wanted my money? After the Belmont Stakes, why did the robbers in the parking want it? I knew how Uncle Louie used the money. But now, my mother had taken it and for what reason?

There were no answers to my questions, and a confused mess of faded pinkish spaghetti streams filled the world.

Without finding answers, I wondered if there was a way to buffer my money from the buzzards. I needed a way to protect myself from robbers in parking lots, and an uncle and a mother who misused money, or from any other person who might try to stop me from achieving my goal.

I heard a voice in my ear. "Arlo, are you still there?" Grant Adams asked.

"Yes. I was just thinking."

"I'm really sorry about what happened, but your mother has legal rights to that account."

"It's okay. Could I ask your advice on something?"

"Sure," Adams answered.

"Is there any way to protect my account from others, so this doesn't happen again?"

The line went quiet for a moment, and then he said, "You might start a company and then have an individual signature on the account. On a standard bank account, a minor needs the signature of an adult. But we could set up a company in a way that an adult doesn't need to co-sign. What do you think?"

We discussed it for a while. The bank had a specialist that managed company setups, so I asked Grant Adams to register a company for me.

"What do you want to call your company?" Adams asked.

A flash went through my thoughts. "Let's call it, Tumbling Oak."

"That's an unusual name."

I said, "I tumbled from the oak tree on our property, so that's what I'd like to call it."

Grant Adams laughed over the phone. "Why not. Tumbling Oak Incorporated. You will be the proud owner of a new company."

A week later I received a large envelope in the mail full of elaborate details about forming a company and opening a bank account. I spent hours carefully reading every word. There were some terms I didn't understand, so I looked them up in the dictionary.

At the same time, I was surprised how much I actually did understand in the documentation. The many hours of reading newspapers had significantly helped my reading abilities, as well as my understanding of financial terms.

I walked five miles to the town post office and sent the paperwork back to Grant Adams, for Tumbling Oak Incorporated.

Now I would have more control over my bank account, and no one could steal from me. Yet, dark storm clouds surrounded me when I thought about what the buzzards can do. And, were there more out there?

CHAPTER 11

I didn't tell Louie what my mother had done, knowing he would empty a bottle of whiskey and then stomp around the backyard screaming things about Iwo Jima. And who knows what he would do to my mother if he tracked her down in San Diego. While considering this, a plan emerged in my mind, and I needed Louie to implement it.

Once the bank account for Tumbling Oak Inc. was opened, I transferred nineteen thousand dollars from our partnership account to the new Tumbling Oak account. There was still one thousand dollars in the joint account I had with my mother. I left it there in case she might need it in the future.

I didn't have feelings toward my mother, realizing there was something different in me than in other people. Most people reacted to events in ways I didn't understand, and I attributed their reactions as emotions.

Whenever I walked into town, I'd sit on a bench at a park where there was a playground. I watched the way children ran to their parents and hugged them, and how they laughed and cried. Those kinds of responses didn't come automatically to me. They hardly came at all. Instead, I saw colors and the colors were not predictable or consistent. If Louie yelled at me, his words might come out as red, whereas they might also be green or silver or blue.

I wondered how I could find out more about emotions as they were not a natural part of my being.

The day the funds were deposited into the Tumbling Oak account I went to Louie and told him I had an idea. Since the death of my grandfather, a golden river had appeared, and it was leading to somewhere.

"Talk to me later," he said.

Much of the time he ignored me, but I knew how to get his

attention. "I have a way of better-guessing cars."

His eyes opened wide, and he looked down at me. "You mean to win more?"

"Yes."

"Well, come on, let's talk about it."

We went out on the front porch and took our regular places. Neither of us ever sat in my grandfather's chair. Louie asked, "What's your idea?"

"I think we need to move to Chicago."

"What?"

"We need to get closer to the C.B.O.T, the Chicago Board of Trade."

"What's that?"

I said, "When you bet on horses is it better to be hundreds of miles away from the racetrack or to be where the horses are running?"

"Don't be stupid. The racetrack is better," he replied.

"Then we need to be closer to the track, at least what we might call the 'futures racetrack.' When we read things in the Los Angeles newspaper, we are always a day late, and that limits our ability to make money. It would be helpful if we were close to the action."

Louie stayed quiet and looked toward the end of the road, as though he was guessing cars. "Chicago? He asked.

"Yes."

"Makes sense. When should we go?"

"Today. We could be in Las Vegas by this evening."

The mention of Las Vegas caught his attention. "Okay, I'll go talk with Carlos and then we can get packed."

Thirty minutes later we headed east.

* * *

In Las Vegas, Louie lost seven hundred dollars playing a variety of different games, like craps, roulette, and blackjack. I could have helped but didn't want him to get distracted. Also, winning too much money in Las Vegas could cause trouble. In the newspaper, I had read that the city was controlled by an organization called The Mafia. Some people said they did wrong things.

We left Las Vegas, and after three days of travel, we were in Chicago. Every weekday, at ten o'clock in the morning a guide gave a tour through the Chicago Board of Trade, so the day after our arrival we joined the tour.

The guide explained that the building was constructed in 1930, and then she led us from room to room. She described how trade orders flowed in from all over the country and quickly reached the trading floor. As she explicated this, I saw thousands of turbulent streams joining together in a swirling lake, and from there, more streams flowed outwards.

Then she took us to the edge of the trading floor, a lively place where there were hundreds of men in suits, yelling and screaming while making signals with their hands. The guide said that this was called open outcry trading.

I didn't react to them like I did with other crowds, like at racetracks where I had to shuffle and look down at the asphalt. Here I didn't really see the pack of people but instead whirling colors much more complicated than horses running around the racetrack.

The tour group left the room, but I stayed on, fascinated by the movement. Somehow, their cries and hand movements blended into colorful waves like California surf. I sensed momentum, a buildup followed by a crescendo that repeated itself over and over.

I stood there for at least fifteen minutes until one of the

traders walked by and asked, "Are you lost?"

"I don't think so," I replied. There was one group of men on the trading floor that seemed extremely animated. I pointed in their direction and asked, "Why are they so excited?"

He looked at the group and then back to me. "Soybeans. There's an oversupply, and the price has dropped like a rock. People are trying to unload their positions."

"But it's going to go in the other direction," I stated.

"I don't think so, but why do you say that."

I saw turquoise waves building from an opposite direction ready to crash across the previous waves that had lost their force. How could I describe this to the man? "Because the price went too far," I said.

"You mean oversold?"

"I guess. If that's what you call it. They overreacted."

His eyes drifted to the soybean traders who were yelling quite loud, and he turned to me and said, "You know, you might be right."

He quickly left me and blended into the group of active men and then I saw him waving his hands in the air, sending signals to other traders with his fingers.

Soon after that Louie found me and said, "You don't belong here. We need to go."

As we left, I knew Louie was wrong. I belonged there, to be close to the real-time ebb and flow of colorful turbulent rivers, swirling lakes and crashing waves.

CHAPTER 12

We stayed in a hotel one block away from the CBOT, and for two months we both got into routines. I liked routines. To some extent, they stabilized me.

Through an advertisement in the newspaper, I found a company that executed trades on the CBOT. It was called F.E.S. for Futures Exchange Services and was run by a guy named Mario Portalini. It was in a building just across the street from the CBOT, so that was ideal for me.

I transferred most of the money from my Tumbling Oak bank account in California to my F.E.S account.

As we settled into our routines, Louie typically stayed out late and got back in the early hours of the morning, if he even got back at all. He was happy as long as he could take money from our partner account. As per our agreement, every time he took out money, I withdrew an equal amount and put it into my Tumbling Oak account at F.E.S.

My routine was to get up early, eat breakfast at the hotel then walk to the CBOT. There I wandered around the trading room. No one gave me any trouble, and I suspected they thought I was the son of one of the traders.

I mainly watched the soybean traders until the direction of the market became apparent, and then I'd walk across the street and take an elevator up five floors to F.E.S.,

Every day Mario greeted me with a big smile, and he'd say, "Hello Mister Arlo. What can we do today?"

In two months of trading my F.E.S. account grew to over ninety thousand dollars.

Then one morning after my visit to the CBOT, I made my way to the offices of F.E.S. Upon exiting the elevator, I immediately sensed something was different. A policeman stood by the front door, and two other men in suits were inside.

I approached the policeman and asked, "Is something

wrong?"

"Who are you?" He asked.

"Arlo Harkin."

"Okay, so what are you doing here?"

"To see Mario."

"Mario?" He peered into the office and said, "Detective. You better talk to this kid."

I stepped into the office and saw that things had changed. The same desk and chair were there, but the file cabinets were open. Papers spread randomly across Mario's desk and on the floor.

One of the detectives looked at me and asked, "Do you know where Mario is?"

"No. He's usually here."

"So, you don't know where he is?"

"No."

"How do you know him?"

"He trades futures for me."

"For you? What do you mean?

"I have an account with him."

"And how much is in the account?

"Ninety-nine thousand dollars."

The detective looked at the other man and then the police officer and said to me, "You're kidding me."

"No. That was the balance of my account yesterday."

The detective scratched his head. "How old are you kid?"

"Thirteen years old."

"Come on, you're jiving with us."

I knew what jiving meant, having seen that word in the newspaper. Louie also used it. "I'm not jiving with you," I replied.

The detective looked at the other men and then at me. "Well kid, I'm sorry to tell you, but your money is likely gone."

"Gone?" I asked.

"Yes, it seems that Mario Portalini was a bucketeer."

"What's that?" I asked.

"He was running this place as a bucket shop."

I didn't understand what that was. "F.E.S. is a brokerage so what is this bucket shop?"

"He's running fake trades. Clients think they are trading in a futures contract, but there is no corresponding transaction at the CBOT. The transaction goes into his bucket, and he takes the opposite side of the trade. In other words, you are not participating in the real market."

When he said that I saw dark clouds. With my ninety-nine thousand dollars controlling millions of dollars of soybean futures, Mario was not able to cover the losses in his bucket. So instead, he took my money and ran away.

The detective said, "What I can't figure out is how a thirteen-year-old kid would have an account with so much money. Something smells fishy."

I didn't know what to say, and I didn't smell fish. The dark clouds turned to the same violet purple as when I thought of Snodgrass and Minx, and like when Louie was spending money like crazy, and like when my mother emptied my bank account

The dark cloud began to swirl with force around us. It wasn't true that something was fishy. I was just using my abilities to make trades, and in no way was I working with Mario. All I did was trust him.

The detective said, "I'm sorry kid, but your story doesn't make sense. Who are your parents?"

"My father died in the war, and my mother lives in San Diego."

"San Diego? Then what are you doing here?"

"Trading the futures market."

The detective turned to his partner and said, "We've got something bizarre here." Then he whispered, "He seems to be abnormal."

The other detective nodded.

The first detective turned to me. "Listen, kid, you should be in school, yet you're giving us some hair-brained story about trading futures. I figure that you know more about Mr. Portalini than you are letting on. We need to find him. We're taking you down to the precinct to ask some questions and to get a social worker involved. If you live in San Diego what are you doing here?"

"I never said I live in San Diego," I countered. "You asked where my parents live."

The detective raised his eyebrows.

At that point, the clouds turned from violet purple to dark gray, and they converged into a river, and it shot forward down the hall. There was an urgency to it, and I didn't hesitate and immediately bolted through the open door and followed it down the hallway and to the emergency stairwell.

The two detectives and the policeman were big bulky men, and as I flew down five floors of stairs, I heard them clomping along behind me. While being naturally wobbly, the countless hours of running the path in the orange grove had made me quick.

Finally, I reached the ground floor, and I zoomed out the front door and sprinted down the sidewalk dodging people. Behind me, I saw the two detectives charge out the front door followed by the policeman. I quickly turned into an alley. Ten minutes later I was back at our hotel.

Louie was sleeping on his bed, and I went to him and shook him.

"Huh," he muttered, slowly opening his bloodshot eyes.

"We've got to go," I stuttered.

"Go where?"

"We need to get out of Chicago?"

"Why? What's going on? I like it here."

"The police are after me."

He slowly sat up, ran his fingers through his hair and said, "What do the police want with you?"

"They think I'm working with Mario?"

"Who's Mario?"

"My futures broker."

He shook his head. "I don't get it."

"It doesn't matter about Mario. They want to take me to the police station and ask me questions. They're wondering why a boy from California would be in Chicago and be working with Mario."

"Okay, okay. So, where do we go from here?"

"We need to get out of Chicago as quickly as possible."

Louie got up from the bed, headed for the bathroom and a minute later I heard the shower turn on.

One hour later we were in our shiny red Ford headed west toward California.

CHAPTER 13

The encounter with the police gave a similar electrical shock as the oak tree, only the color was different. It was surprising how quickly I acted, and the black river still sent vibrations, only now there were red zigzags resembling lightning flashes.

I considered why I had these reactions. People felt fear. Is that what it was?

Or, maybe it was something different? Was I reacting to the loss of my money? Then, I sat up in the car seat with a consideration that perhaps it wasn't so easy to think and grow rich because people continually stopped me from achieving this goal. An image of Mario hovered over me like a buzzard.

In the past, if I couldn't reach the end of the swimming pool and tap the tiles three times, and spit, my body trembled, and I would hum and even holler. Not being able to touch the oak tree was a blockage to my routines, and that gave me internal quakes.

Mario had taken my money, and that was another kind of blockage, so now, what could I do?

I still had five hundred dollars in my Tumbling Oak Inc. bank account in California and one thousand in the joint account with my mother. Louie and I had fifty thousand in our partner account, but he was spending it faster than I could make it.

The thought of starting over sent an image of giant claws gripping my body and pulling me into a tiny dark room with no exit. Every time I made money it was taken away from me. A question came to my mind. Should I continue with the goal of think and grow rich? But, what else was I capable of doing?

It was complicated, and life was now like a game of Pick-Up-Sticks. With some moves, you successfully remove a stick from the pile. Then, the next move brought the pile down.

My pile kept crumbling, and it obstructed my goal to think and grow rich.

Should I choose another goal? The answer was no, because this one made logical sense.

With that thought, I had an idea. Our horizon was unknown, but a river appeared. We needed to go another way.

I said, "Louie, we need to head east."

"What for? Let's get back to California."

"I had a fascinating experience back at Mario's office."

"I'm still not sure who this Mario is."

"I told you. He is this bucket shop person that makes trades look like real trades, but they are not real. He took all my money."

"Well, I certainly wouldn't use the word fascinating."

"You don't understand. What was fascinating was that I saw this dark thing. It shot out in front of me, and I immediately reacted and followed it."

"I don't get it," he said.

"The dark thing has now turned from black to green, and it's curving around and headed east. We need to go east."

"Arlo, you're really spooky. Let's go back to California,"

I knew how to convince Louie and said, "Remember what I said about being close to the action, like being close to the horses?"

"Ah, yeah?"

"We need to go to New York because the big-daddy of all racetracks is in New York."

"You mean the Belmont Racetrack. It's not. The big-daddy is Churchill Downs in Kentucky."

"No. There's something bigger than both of them combined."

"What's that?"

"The New York Stock Exchange.

He drove the car off the road and onto in a wide rest area, turned the engine off and sat there without saying anything.

Finally, he said, "You know, you might have an interesting idea. Belmont Racetrack is close by and New York City is known for its nightclubs."

When he said that the green flow turned blackish. I said, "Nightclubs cause you to stomp around and scream when you get home, and you remember what happened at Belmont Park. If we go to New York City, please promise that you won't go to those places."

He looked at me and smiled like his cheeks were breaking, only it didn't go to his eyes. "Okay, Arlo. Let's get to know the Big Apple."

Louie started the car, and we headed east. When I looked at the road in front of us, it was a pale green color like leaves in the early spring.

Every time I glanced at Louie, the pale green swirled off from the road like misty fog transforming into a dark purple.

Was I right to insist on New York City, or should we have gone back to California?

* * *

Three days after leaving Chicago we checked into a hotel in New York City.

Louie wanted to stay at the Waldorf Astoria because it had the most beautiful 'birds,' but it was five miles away from the New York Stock Exchange. It seemed strange to me that a hotel would have birds, but then I figured out that he was again using an expression and was talking about ladies. You learn a lot from reading newspapers.

In the end, I convinced him to be close to the action, so we got a hotel just off Broadway, a few blocks away from the exchange.

In New York City, we got into routines pretty quick. Chicago had taught me to not use the services of the first broker I saw in the newspaper. At the New York Stock Exchange, they gave out a list of qualified brokers, and I chose Lehman Brothers because they had survived the Great Depression.

At Lehman Brothers, we opened two accounts, one for our partner account and one for Tumbling Oak.

Every morning, I'd eat breakfast at the hotel while reading the stock page in the New York Times

I discovered that with some stocks you could bet on something called 'options.' They were in some ways similar to futures. That's where the most money could be made, and that's where I concentrated.

After reading the morning newspaper, I'd walk two blocks to the New York Stock Exchange and tag along with some men in suits, trying to look like I belonged with them. Then I'd watch the market open while looking for points of energy and flows in the large trading room. Then I'd walk across the street to Lehman Brothers and make my trades.

The amount in both our accounts grew and especially in the Tumbling Oak account. After one month, it increased to sixty thousand dollars.

There was one thing that gave me electric shocks and made me wobbly. It was the attention given to me by the people at Lehman Brothers. Folks working there stopped what they were doing and stared at me. I heard one man call me, "the wonder kid." After that, I began to imagine some of those people as buzzards so didn't go into their offices anymore. Instead, I called my broker with the telephone in our hotel room.

In fact, the turbulence of New York City brought unsettling storms of metallic reds and canary yellows, and the small confines of our hotel room pushed in on me like a shrinking cage around a prisoner. I thought about going back to our orange farm and then I got an idea from reading ads in the newspaper. It would help me to have a solitude place for thinking, like our newspaper room back home. For that, we needed our own house or apartment.

It was easy to convince Louie about my idea because he was also fed up with living at the hotel. So, I talked with my broker at Lehman Brothers, and he said we could buy whatever we wanted, and he would arrange a loan. Although, he said there were risks by leveraging too much in real estate.

On this, I suspected he had logic. Guessing cars and horses and stocks was one thing, but buying an apartment was different and entirely new to me. It caused me to wonder if Louie and I might be creating problems for ourselves.

CHAPTER 14

We looked at three places and then bought an apartment called a penthouse. At first, that name concerned me, because I didn't like the idea of being pent-up like in a chicken coop. But, it wasn't like that at all. The apartment was at the top of a tall building, had four bedrooms, three bathrooms, and there were full-time guards at the front door downstairs. Our apartment overlooked Central Park and had a view of the city.

Because of the height of the building, it was difficult for me to look out the window for it made me dizzy and the multitude of lights at night was like an attack.

Louie bought a lot of furniture for the apartment, to make it comfortable, but in my room, we kept it simple with a bed, a table, a large book rack, and a soft lounge chair where I spent evenings reading newspapers and books.

In the afternoons, I walked in Central Park or sat on park benches where I pondered on the endless colorful streams coming from the trees and people.

It was Fall, and the trees had different colors than those in our orange grove, although our oak tree turned red and brown during that time of year.

With the use of options, my Tumbling Oak account was rapidly growing, but our partnership account was something different. Louie was liberally spending it.

Our schedules differed, and we only saw each other for brief moments during any twenty-four-hour period. He slept during the day, and I slept at night.

One day I was looking out the window of our apartment at Central Park, and a green river interested me. I followed it into the elevator, downstairs, and across the street. I walked into the park, and it disappeared at a bench, so I sat down and waited.

It was a warm autumn day, and I felt the sun filter through

the green leaves of the trees. People strolled by, and I noticed an older woman walking in my direction. She had a straight posture, and there was something like elegance in the way she carried her trim figure.

She held a brown paper bag in her left hand and sat on a bench opposite from me. Even before she opened the bag, pigeons gathered at her feet. From the bag, she took out a handful of popcorn and threw it on the ground. More pigeons arrived, and they began to fight over the popcorn.

She saw me looking at her, and she smiled and said, "The popcorn doesn't have salt or butter, much better for the birds."

I hadn't thought of that. Then some gray-brown sparrows showed up and were battling with the pigeons. The sparrows were faster than the pigeons, and they darted in and stole the popcorn before the pigeons could get there.

I said, "They look hungry."

She laughed. "I come here every day, yet they are never satisfied."

I didn't answer but instead stared at the birds while thinking of what she said, "They are never satisfied." That statement created an unusual formation in my mind consisting of the same colors of the birds with grays, blues, and browns overlaying the green river.

What was unusual was how the river shot forward and then turned dark and ended by going over a crevice. I wasn't sure what to make of it. Maybe it meant that a quest for satisfaction ends nowhere, or perhaps something else.

I was interrupted from my thoughts when the woman asked, "Are you okay?"

My eyes looked up to the trees. "What do you mean?"

"I'm sorry, but you looked disturbed by something."

"Not really," I replied.

"Please forgive me," she said, "but it seemed you were sad, or reflective."

"What do you mean?" I asked.

She smiled. "Oh, it's just something I do. I observe body language."

"Body language?"

"Yes, the way people move and what that communicates. Body gestures and expressions convey more than words."

That was interesting, like finding a new stock to invest in. "How do you know that?" I asked.

"It's part of my profession. For some years I've been a teacher at the New York School of Acting. Actors need to know these things."

It was fascinating to hear that a body could communicate, and I wanted to know more. "What did my body language tell you?" I asked.

"Well, that you were reflecting on something in a deep way and it seemed to trouble you. It made you feel odd, for lack of a better term."

I looked up at the trees and said, "Yes, I was thinking about things, about what you said about never being satisfied. But, I wasn't feeling odd or even feeling anything."

"What do you mean?"

"I don't have feelings."

She blinked, and her eyes opened wide. "That's highly unusual," she replied. "Could you tell me about it? Because of my profession, this interests me, but I don't mean to pry."

She seemed honest, so I told her. "Some years ago, I realized that I don't act the same way as others, like being sad or happy. It just doesn't happen in me."

She nodded. "That's uncommon. Emotions are a natural part human reaction, yet I suppose it's possible that some people have unique responses."

"I see emotions in other people. I just don't feel them." One bird began to peck at a smaller one like he was the boss.

She asked, "Do you feel pain, like if you stub your toe or smash your finger."

"Yes. That I physically feel, but not the other kind of emotional stuff."

"You mentioned not feeling sadness or happiness. What about love? Have you ever experienced that?"

Her question had never crossed my mind. "No. I'm not sure. I don't know what love is."

"Oh my," she replied.

She stared at me, and I saw a rose-colored hue appear above her head. I looked at the trees, and the green river was back and flowing, and it triggered an idea. Could she teach one thing I was missing? Surely once learned, it might enable me to better reach my goal.

I asked, "You said you teach acting?"

"Yes."

"Do you take students?"

"Well, not now. I'm taking time off, for health reasons."

"Would you take one student?"

"What do you mean?"

"I'd like you to teach me to act."

She laughed. "Act what?"

I stared down the path. "Like I said, to teach me to act."

Her jaw dropped a bit, and she peered into my face. "Well, I suppose we could spend a few hours learning some basics."

"No," I said. "I want to hire you every afternoon."

"What do you mean by hire?"

"I'll pay you to teach me."

"I can't do that," she stated.

"Yes, you can. How much would it cost?"

"No. I can't".

"How much?

She paused for a moment and asked, "Why do you want to learn how to act?"

"For personal reasons."

"Most people learn to act to be in the movies or on stage, if they are lucky enough to get a part."

"Never," I exclaimed. "I'd never ever want to be in the movies!"

"So, why learn acting?"

"There's something I'd like to learn."

"And what is it?"

"Can you teach me to act normal?"

The woman stayed silent for a moment, took a deep breath and said, "Wow. That's the first time I've heard that one."

"Well, can you? Can you teach me to act normal?" I asked.

She hesitated then said, "I guess I can give you a few hours of coaching."

"I can pay," I said.

She laughed. "How about fifty cents for one afternoon?"

"I don't want one afternoon." I reached into my front pocket, pulled out some dollars and held it toward her. "You can have this much each week."

She reluctantly took the money and counted it. "That's four hundred dollars."

"That's right. Four hundred a week for the first month. If the teaching works, then there'll be more for the coming months."

"I can't believe this," she said. "I came here to enjoy the birds and how I'm hired to teach. Where did you get this money? It's too much for someone to be carrying around in Central Park."

"What's wrong with Central Park?" I asked.

"Robbers. They are everywhere in New York City."

I thought of the two men who had robbed us at Belmont Park and how they hit Louie, and he fell to the ground. "How much is the right amount to carry?" I asked.

She didn't answer, but said, "I can't take this."

"I want to learn to act to be normal," I insisted.

She looked at the birds in front of her as they waited expectantly for the next serving of popcorn. She took a deep breath and when she exhaled there was a translucent fog that surrounded her, and it seemed like something was broken.

She reached into her large bag and took out a business card and handed it to me. On it was her name, Maria Sanchez, and underneath her name, it said, "Acting Coach."

She looked at me and said, "This is a highly unusual request to act normal. I need to consider what that means, for what is normal?"

CHAPTER 15

The following afternoon I walked to Maria Sanchez's apartment, which was five blocks away from my place. I avoided looking at people but kept my head down while observing the cracks in the sidewalk. That was a way to avoid the turmoil of the city.

The words in Maria's question didn't go away but kept spinning around me like hula hoops, which were now becoming so popular with kids. She had asked, "What is normal?"

When looking at the sidewalk, one could say it was all sidewalk, but none of it was normal. Each sidewalk was different. In fact, each step you take leads to a different sidewalk universe, some parts of it having long cracks, or little cracks, or with various colors and stains, or parts where you have to tip-toe around dog poops and gum and bird droppings and cigarette butts. Would it be possible to describe a normal sidewalk?

People were much more complicated than sidewalks, So, Maria's question had logic. What is normal? Is there really a *normal* person? Maybe I was asking her to teach me something that didn't exist?

Her apartment was on the second floor of an old brown five-story building. The elevator was out of order, so I walked up the stairs and knocked on the door.

She let me in and invited me to sit on a wooden chair with a cushion on it.

She said, "It is better you sit there for on the couch it's not as easy to practice movements."

"That's fine," I said, as her chair was more comfortable than my chair on our porch in California.

I looked around her living room, and two walls had bookshelves that went from the ceiling to the floor, and they were crammed with books. The other two walls were entirely covered with pictures in picture frames. Some seemed like photos of families or of Maria growing up, whereas others were of people smiling. Many had signatures on them. A couple of faces were familiar, as I had seen them in the movies.

Most often when I was confronted with so much complexity, it caused me to close my eyes, but a soft gray mist circulated through the room which mitigated the attack from so much information.

I zeroed in on one photo of Maria as a young woman wearing a flowing red dress and on her head and shoulders was a light lace scarf held in place by a large comb on her head.

She said, "That picture was taken in 1939 for a movie I was in."

"You were in the movies?" I asked.

She smiled. "Many. There was always a need for people with Spanish accents and for dancers. I lived in Hollywood for some years before coming to New York for the Broadway shows and then on to London after the war."

"Was it hard to learn the Spanish accent?" I asked.

She laughed. "Not at all. I was born in Spain. It was an impoverished country, so my parents moved to the United States when I was young."

The photos were like the summary of someone's life, each picture a story of its own, yet a soft gray mist blended all into a connected history. The history was trying to tell me something, but I didn't have time to explore it because the lesson needed to begin.

"What do I need to learn?" I asked.

She snapped her fingers and said, "You must learn the first essential. Look at me."

"Huh?" I asked.

"Look at people when you talk to them, not at the pictures or the floor. Yesterday you mostly looked at the trees and birds. Look at people in the eyes, or look at their face. It tells them you are listening and are interested in them."

"But, I'm not always interested."

"I know. Me too. But if you want to be normal, or communicate with others at a basic level, you need to force yourself to look at them."

I tried to look at her as she talked, but it was easier to look at a picture frame on the wall."

"No Arlo," she said. "Look at me." She held up the index finger and middle finger on her right hand and pointed them at her eyes.

I tried, but it was difficult. Finally, I looked at her eyes.

"Now say something, she commanded.

"Like what?" I asked.

"Don't stare. Use expression."

"What is an expression?" I asked.

"It's movements of your face, like this when you are surprised, and this when you are sad, and this when you are happy." She moved her face in different ways. "Now try being happy."

Of course, I had observed those expressions in other people all my life but wasn't sure how to do them correctly. I attempted to look happy.

She slightly nodded her head and said, "Arlo, this is going to take some practice. Are you sure you want to do this?"

"Yes."

"It might take time."

"I don't care," I stated. "I want to learn it."

"Then focus," she demanded.

* * *

Maria spent days trying to teach me facial expressions. Back at my apartment, I'd practice by looking in the mirror. At first, it was hard to make the expressions. More challenging was to know when to use them.

What are the cues in other people that lead you to use an expression? And how can you use the expression without seeming artificial?

Maria was patient, and after a month of work, she said I was making progress. Then we began to practice specific settings, like going to a restaurant, carrying on a conversation, what to ask and not say, how to answer, and how to move your face and body.

One day we were in Central Park, and we saw a young man and young woman walking together. The man's arm was around the young woman's waist, and her head was on his shoulder. They were bundled up because of the cold weather.

"When you see that, how does it make you feel?" Maria asked.

I looked at the couple again and said, "I don't feel anything. Maybe cold."

"Really, no feelings? Nothing that strikes as love?"

"No. I see colors."

Maria was silent and said, "That's fascinating. What colors do you see?"

"Pinks and reds like in a rose garden, but floating on a cloud."

Maria smiled. "Perhaps those colors are feelings?"

I shook my head back and forth as she had taught me. "I'm not sure. Tomorrow, with the same couple I might see purple or blue. So, if colors are feelings, then they are not always consistent."

She raised her eyebrows and said, "Maybe that's the way we experience feelings. It's not fixed chemistry where we always get the same result. Emotions and feelings are volatile."

She could be right, but I knew my colors were not exclusive to feelings. "My colors are more like patterns and designs that sometimes lead to predictions."

"Is that so," she replied, reaching across and taking my hand. "Arlo, what colors do you see when you look at me."

It wasn't so much looking at her as it was her words and the touch of her hand. "I see a design."

"What does that mean?"

"I see pastels in delicately balanced graphics, yet there's something dark in the background."

"Dark?"

"It's like a hand or giant baseball mitt."

"And what is the hand about to do?" She asked.

I didn't want to tell her, but my grandfather said it was best to be honest. "It seems the hand is about to crush the design."

She looked down, and then her eyes became red. Tears went down her cheeks. After taking a deep breath, she said, "Arlo, there's something wrong with me. I'm sick and may not live much longer."

I put on my sad face, and she laughed. "You're a good

student, but still have learning to do." Her words were like colorful bubbles.

For some reason, the dark hand crushing the pastel image made it difficult for me to look her in the eyes, so I said, "Can I help?"

"No. It involves a costly operation."

"What is it?" I asked.

"I have a congenital heart problem. All my years of dancing and exercise kept me in shape, but now it has caught up with me. I need a heart operation."

I gave her my biggest smile but wasn't sure it was appropriate. "It's no problem. Let's get it done."

She did something between a cry and a laugh and said, "We also need to put in more work on your smile. It was a bit overdone."

That meant I needed lots more hours in front of the mirror to master the smile. Therefore, Maria's help was needed, and I couldn't allow her to die. Sometimes logic is easy. "Let's find the best doctors in the world to do this operation," I stated.

CHAPTER 16

We found the best doctor in New York and at the beginning of 1959, Maria had her open-heart operation at the Presbyterian Hospital.

She had something called a heart murmur, which is a hole somewhere in your heart. I looked it up in a book in the library which explained all the technical details. Maria's heart murmur was there since she was a child, but in the past years, it had been getting worse. The doctor said she would die without the operation.

The operation fixed the problem and doctor said it would take time for the repaired pieces to heal. Three days after the surgery I visited her in the hospital.

The Presbyterian Hospital was a large place with a lot of people scurrying around, and it took time to find her room. I walked in, and she was propped up on her bed sipping some juice from a straw. I bought flowers for her, for it seems that's what you are supposed to do when you visit people in the hospital.

I put on my best smile.

She placed the glass of juice on a tray and said, "Arlo, you are getting better, but there's still something wrong. You don't stick your teeth out like a bunny rabbit."

"Like how then?" I asked.

"Like this." She smiled. "You see, I am genuinely happy to see you. I'm not acting. This is natural. Please come here." She held out her arms, and I walked to her, and she gave me a hug. I had to hold the flowers up in the air, so they didn't get squashed.

"How are you?" I asked. It was an important question she had taught me.

"Perfect. I'll be out of here in a week. I'm so thankful to you for enabling this to happen."

"So, we can start the acting lessons again?" I asked.

Maria laughed. "Of course. I owe you a lot."

"I know."

She smiled and said, "I think we also need to work a bit more on your personal skills."

"How is that," I asked.

"Do you feel anything toward me? Are you glad the operation went well?"

"Of course, I'm glad because without the operation you would be dead and then I would never learn to act normal."

"That's what I'm talking about. You need to show empathy."

"What's empathy?"

"It means you have feelings about other people and that you care for them."

"But, I don't have feelings."

"Arlo, I must teach you how to show emotions and empathy if you want to appear normal."

I nodded my head like she had previously taught me, hoping it was the appropriate behavior.

"Arlo, don't overdo it. You look like one of those noddy-dolls."

I slowed down the movement of my head and asked, "Like this?"

She nodded back. "Better."

We talked some more and then she said she was getting tired and needed rest, so I walked away. Before leaving the room, I turned and looked at her. Her eyes were already closed, and I saw the same colors around her from before, only this time the dark cloudy mitt was far away in the background, but it was still there.

* * *

When I got back to our apartment, Louie was awake, sitting at the kitchen table in his bathrobe with a cup of coffee in his hand. His hair was out of place, and his eyes were red. When I looked closer, I saw that he had a cut on his cheek and around his left eye it was purple and swollen.

I smiled when I saw him.

Louie's face stayed frozen. "Well, I'll be darned. I think that's the first time I ever saw you smile. That was strange."

"Why was it strange?

"Two reasons. First, you've never smiled, so there must be something wrong with you. Second, the smile was weird, like a cartoon character or something."

That confirmed more practice was needed. "Did something happen to you?" I asked.

Louie looked down at the ground. "Damn Iwo Jima. I took out a loan to pay off some bets and then lost that."

"Grandfather said not to use that word."

"Okay, okay." He put his elbows on the table and then rested his head in his hands. "Kid, I got a problem. Some dangerous men are after me unless I pay them off."

"How much?"

"I emptied most of our partner account, but still owe fifty thousand dollars."

"What?"

"Yeah. Fifty grand."

"Where do we get it?" I asked. Purple clouds emerged, which was becoming the norm with Louie.

"No idea," he said. "All I know is that they are going to hurt us, you and me if the money ain't paid back. These guys don't mess around. They could take our lives."

Maria had taught me well, for Louie's body language communicated that he was troubled, the way his back bent and the furrow lines on his forehead. "Can we kill them first?" I asked.

Louie's eyes became wide. "Are you crazy? That's the Mafia. If you kill one, you take on an army."

That was interesting for I knew about them. "The newspapers say they own Las Vegas."

"Arlo, I'm serious. These are horrible people."

I thought about that for a second and wondered what these Mafia people could do to us. If they did something to us, then it would stop me from attaining my goal, not only to think and grow rich but now learning to act normal. "Okay. I'll give you the money, but then we need to talk."

"Talk about what."

"About your body language."

"Huh? What's this body language business?"

"It means your movements, about what you are doing every

night."

"What does that have to do with this body language stuff?"

"Everything."

"You are one weird kid."

Words flowed from his mouth like spaghetti streams each one with its unique color and shape. The word weird was fascinating like an orange thistle head. I focused on it, watching its movement as it grew larger and then slowly moved across the room. It dissipated with a small remnant sticking to the wall and oozing down to the floor.

"Arlo, are you listening to me?"

His words were back to their usual sizes. "Listening to you?"

"Yeah."

"You need to do something," I stated.

"Like what?"

"You need to change."

Louie was usually a fighter and often liked to argue, but this time something was different. He nodded his head, and I carefully observed how he was doing it, slow, deliberate, his eyes closed. I figured that's how you acted if you felt remorse. It was a different kind of nod than when you agreed to something. Practicing both types would be good. "There's one thing I need to know," I stated.

"What's that?

"Why are you always talking about the Japs and Iwo Jima whenever you get upset?"

Louie put his head back into his hands and said, "What a horrible question."

I looked at the way his head rested in his hands, his fingers spread, eyes shut, fingers in his hair, shoulders hunched, and two of his fingers tapping his head like a low beat on bongo drums. That's something I needed to learn. Maria would smile when I showed her these new movements.

CHAPTER 17

The following morning, I walked into Lehman Brothers rather than calling them on the telephone. I asked my broker for fifty thousand dollars. He said it would take thirty minutes to get it.

While waiting for the money, we talked about the stock markets, and he stated that the 1950's had been a bull market, which meant share prices were going up.

He said, "I've been watching your portfolio since you opened it and, I've never seen such an outstanding performance. But, your uncle has been taking significant risk."

"I understand that," I said. When I had opened the account, I told my broker that I was following the advice of my uncle, who was following the predictions of different market newsletters. He didn't know that I was the one making the decisions.

"All bull markets come to an end. By putting everything into futures and options, you carry high risk, and you could end up losing much of your fortune."

"It's just money," I said, slightly smiling as Maria had taught me, while carefully looking to see his body language reaction.

He shook his head. "I'm afraid it's not that easy. You'd go on an emotional roller coaster if you lost that much money."

He didn't know that my emotions would feel very little. I smiled again, wondering if I was overdoing it. I said, "If we see any signs of a market downturn, then we can adjust the risk."

"That's easy to say, but market downturns can happen extremely fast, so there's no time to react."

A man walked in with a fancy cardboard box with Lehman Brothers written on the side, and from it, he counted out twenty bound bundles of hundred-dollar bills, five thousand dollars in each bundle.

He left, and my broker said, "Do you want to count it?"

"No thank you," I said. "I'll just take it." I had brought two large brown paper grocery bags with me and put the bundles in the bags. When they were full, I covered them with newspapers.

I noticed his eyes getting big. He said, "You mean you're just going to walk out on the street with all that money?"

"My uncle is waiting for me." Louie was at the apartment.

"You like to live dangerously," he said.

I hadn't thought of that. My primary objective was to get the money to Uncle Louie, so he could pay off the Mafia loan shark people. Now, my broker's words triggered off a warning. I thought of the individuals who had stolen money from me and didn't want it to happen again, yet here I was taking risk.

Red and yellow lightning bolts flashed, like the ones in the parking lot at the racetrack. The flashing made me dizzy.

I lifted the two bags and shuffled toward the elevator.

* * *

Louie and I took a taxi to an area of New York City called the Bronx. I thought that was an excellent name and told myself to look it up the next time I went to the library.

Louie instructed the taxi to stop in front of a rundown office building, and he said to me, "You wait here."

"I'm coming," I said.

"No, you're not," Louie commanded.

"Yes, I am. It's my money, and I want to learn where it goes."

Louie hesitated, then paid the taxi driver, and we went into the office building and down a hall. "Don't say a word when we are in there. Do you understand?"

"Why not?"

"Because these guys are wicked. I should never have accepted their loan."

"But, you couldn't stop yourself, right? Because of your addiction."

"Addiction? What do you mean?"

"It's just like alcohol. You don't know when to stop."

Louie looked at me, and his cheeks became red. It was remarkable how I was starting to notice body language.

After the fall from my grandfather's oak tree I saw details in everything, but for some reason, I had never actually observed them in peoples' expressions.

Until Maria's teaching, I avoided looking at people. Now, in Louie's face I sensed that the redness was not caused by anger, but by shame, for the look on his face triggered light purple clouds.

Louie nodded and said, "Let's get this over with."

At the end of the hallway was a wooden door and Louie knocked on it, and we entered. There was a desk, and behind it, a man sat on a chair while holding a cigar in one hand. With the other hand, he held a telephone to his ear. On a chair at the side of the room was another man. He was massive with a neck so big that it seemed his head was directly attached to his shoulders.

The man put down the telephone. He smiled, but it was tight and not nice looking. "Hello, Louie. Who's the kid?"

"My nephew. I'm his guardian."

I noticed that Louie didn't tap his head with his pointy finger like he sometimes did when he introduced me to people.

"Hi, kid. I'm Al. What's your name?" The man asked.

"Can you teach me to smile like that?"

"Huh? Wha-da-ya mean?"

"When we came in you smiled. It wasn't a happy smile or a nice to see you kind of smile. It's like there was meanness in the smile."

"Huh?"

"Yes, I'd like to learn to smile like that. You see, I'm learning body language."

"What?" Al looked at Louie and asked, "What's wrong with this kid?

The large man without a neck smirked and put his hand over

his mouth, his chest bouncing up and down. I pointed at him and said, "You see, that's a real smile because he thinks something's funny. I can do that one. But, your smile had teeth in it, yet there was also ugliness. It's like your cheeks were tight, but your eyebrows were down as you stared from underneath them."

The large man was now bouncing up and down, laughter rising from his throat.

Al commanded, "Georgio, stop."

"I can't boss. It's too funny. The kid's right. You got an intimidating smile."

That was a right word, intimidating. Maybe Maria could teach me how to do an intimidating smile.

Al's face became stiff, and he glared at Louie and said, "Louie, you got my money? If you owe money you gotta pay or you suffer the consequences."

Louie stepped forward and placed the two paper bags on Al's desk.

As Al reached for the bags, I said, "You know, I'm going to practice that stiff face, but it would be really nice if you could teach it to me." Somehow, I was hung up on that smile, and my mind was in a loop.

Georgio was howling, deep grunts coming from the depths of his chest.

Then I noticed something odd. The colors emanating from Al were similar to those of Mario in Chicago. I said, "Could I ask you something?"

"I've had enough of you," Al said.

"Do you know Mario Portalini who ran a bucket shop in Chicago?"

Both Al and Georgio became still. The slate gray color of recognition emanated from both of them.

"What if I do?" Al asked.

"Tell him that he owes me money? You just said that if you

owe money you gotta pay or you suffer the consequences. And you tell him that the next time I see him, I'll give him the stiff smile."

Georgio laughed again, wheezing sounds coming deep from his chest. "This kid's too much."

Al smiled in a more regular way. "When I see Mario, I'll tell him you're looking for him. And I agree that if he owes you money, he better pay or suffer the consequences. He owes me money too."

"Thank you," I said.

Al looked at Louie and asked, "Who is this kid again?"

"My nephew. His name is Arlo.

CHAPTER 18

We left the Mafia office, and I thought that Al and Georgio didn't seem like such horrible people. Anyway, I figured that Al was loaning money just like banks loan money.

At the end of the street was a coffee shop, so we went inside, found a booth in a corner and sat down. Louie ordered a coffee, and I ordered chocolate milk and a Danish pastry.

After the waitress left us, Louie spoke with a quiet voice, "I thought I told you not to say anything."

"But I wanted to learn his body language, and I read in the newspaper that you don't get anything without asking." I was still thinking about Al's behavior, not only his smile but his hand movements and the tone of his voice. The sound of his English was different from people in California. In California, the spaghetti strands of words were long and rounded. His were zig-zaggy.

"Even so, you don't mess with guys like that," Louie stated.

"Then why'd you go to them in the first place?"

Louie put his hands on the table and then interlaced his fingers, as though he was going to pray, although I'd never seen him pray. He said, "I was desperate. I lost a lot of money in a gambling house, and I stupidly thought I could win it back."

"But you didn't, and then you used all the money in our partner account, and you came to me for the rest."

Louie raised his praying hands to his forehead and said, "Yes. I'm a fool."

"Why do you do it?"

He slowly put his hands back on the table. "Do what?

The waitress brought our order, and when she walked away, I replied. "Why do you do it? Why do you drink so much alcohol, and stay out all night and gamble?" I was curious and really wanted to know.

He was quiet for a moment, then said, "It's a mystery." I think I do it to forget."

"Forget what?"

"I went through a horrible experience in the war." He shook his head, poured sugar into his coffee and slowly stirred it with a spoon.

"I'd like to know what happened," I stated.

"It's difficult to talk about."

"Please tell me."

He took a sip of his coffee. "Your father got a draft letter. That means the government demands that you join the army and go to war. I decided to go with him and even though I was barely seventeen they took me. Somehow, we thought the Marines were more exciting than the army. After basic training at Camp Pendleton, we took a long ride on a ship and then we floated for a couple of weeks off an island called Iwo Jima while the Navy shot bombs onto the island. Then the generals decided to attack. We got in boats and stormed the beaches, and that's when all hell broke loose."

He took another sip of his coffee while I bit into my Danish roll.

"What happened?" I asked.

"As I said, all hell broke loose. The Japs were well fortified, and all the bombing didn't achieve its purpose. It was the most awful thing you could ever imagine, and tens of thousands of soldiers were killed and wounded, on both sides. We imagined that the Japanese were monsters, but they were just a bunch of scared kids like we were. They had been told that we were cannibals. Your father and I fought side by side, and you can picture how we felt, two young guys whose entire world had been a rural orange farm."

That was the first time I ever heard Louie refer to them as Japanese rather than Japs and indeed I did picture the event even more than Louie would think. "Is that where my father died?" I asked, taking a drink of my chocolate milk.

Louie hung his head. "We fought together side by side and hundreds of guys were going down all around us. Finally, he took a bullet, and I'm thankful he died instantly. Think how it was for me to lose my older brother, my best friend. An hour after that I took a bullet in the hip and was evacuated and then was out of action for the rest of the war. And that was it."

I was struggling to feel Louie's feelings, but couldn't. At the same time, I understand how he carried that with him. He was now twenty-nine years old. That had not been a good experience for him, and I wondered if this would limit him for the rest of his life? "You got a purple heart," I stated.

"Yeah, and a messed-up head. You know, the stupidest thing about Iwo Jima? The whole thing was a waste. All those soldiers killed and wounded, and our military never really used the place. They said it was strategic, but the war quickly moved on to other places, and they just used the island's runway for a few emergency landings. It shows you the wisdom of governments.

They are worse than the Mafia for their stupid decisions bring a lot more heartache."

"Is that why you sometimes talk about stupid Iwo Jima."

"Yes. I guess it's a way of expressing a lot of things and one of them is the collective stupidity of those in political power. In the end, the lives of everyday people mean nothing. Don't trust the government." He took a deep breath and stared at me. "Don't ever forget that Arlo."

I finished my pastry and chocolate milk while the waitress brought a refill of coffee for Louie. The thought of Iwo Jima and my father's death seemed abstract, yet there were fireworks as I considered that event, explosions of colors with the screams of ghost-like people in the background. The images were remarkable, a sight I hadn't seen before.

When my chocolate milk was finished, I asked, "So, are you going to keep staying out all night and doing the things you do?"

Louie looked me in the eyes and said, "I don't know. Right now, it's a habit I can't break."

"You have to. Otherwise, you will die." A black mitt drifted in the background.

Both of Louie's hands encircled his coffee cup, and that's where his eyes focused for a long time, as though he was contemplating what I said. Finally, he looked up and said, "Arlo, you are barely a teen, but you act and reason like you're fifty. You're right. I need to get free from the insidious prison of my behavior."

I understood that. I was also geared to habits, routines that worked their way into my soul. Running back and forth to the oak tree was only one example. The power of the tree was just too strong to break.

But, it appeared that some habits had unwanted results. I had read that alcohol can destroy your body and gambling can be just as bad. An idea came to me, and I asked, "Would you like to stop?"

He nodded. "That would be the best thing."

"In the newspaper, I read about a clinic in upstate New York that helps people. It's called the Hope Center or something like that. Why don't you go there for a while to see if they can help?"

"Sounds like an insane asylum."

"It might be, but at least one member of the family could experience one of those places."

Louie laughed. "Arlo, I always thought it would be you. How the world plays strange tricks."

CHAPTER 19

We made the arrangements, and Louie's biggest worry was who was going to take care of me during the month he was gone. It was no big deal, as I had been taking care of myself for several months.

Louie got into our red Ford and drove off to upstate New York. I waved, and he waved back, and the car floated down a green river although far in the distance the river disappeared into a darkish, swamp-like green mist.

After Louie drove off, I knew I could now focus on my routine of reading the stock market results and visiting the NYSE and calling Lehman Brothers, and acting lessons with Maria. I needed to make up the fifty thousand dollars paid to Al, who had become another buzzard in my life. And, I had to make up for the money spent on Maria's heart operation, although I didn't see her as a buzzard. And, I needed to restart our partner account, which Louie had drained to almost nothing.

It was the afternoon, so I went to Maria's place. She was doing much better after her heart operation, and every day she was taking long walks in Central Park.

After knocking on the door, she opened it and gave me a hug. It was an odd sensation, pastel rosebuds, yet I still saw the dark mitt hovering in the sky far in the background.

"How are you, Arlo?" She asked. "I haven't seen you for a few days."

"I had to take care of a few things for my uncle. He got in trouble with the Mafia, and I had to help him. Everything is okay now."

She had a small grin. "Arlo, are you imagining things?"

She had never met Uncle Louie and didn't know the life he lived. "No. It happened. In fact, I met a man called Al, and he used some body language that another other man called intimidating. His face was a smile that wasn't a smile, something like this."

I tried to copy what Al had done, tight cheeks drawing the mouth open, head slightly tilted forward, eyes squinting under heavy eyebrows.

"Oh, I see," Maria said. "That's probably not the most helpful of expressions."

"I want to learn it," I said.

She shook her head. "Arlo, you never stop surprising me."

We worked on acting out body language for a while, and occasionally I glanced at the photos on Maria's walls.

One photo had an actor called David Niven. He was British, and Maria had met him when she was in stage plays and musicals in London. I pointed at the photo and asked, "Do you ever miss acting?"

"Absolutely, and I miss London. Those were good times just before the war. Then, a lot of the city got bombed by the Nazis, but the British have been rebuilding. I was also there after the war for a couple of years. I'd love to go back there someday, and now that my heart is fixed I just might do it."

I visualized what London would be like, with cars driven on

the wrong side of the road, two story busses and people with funny accents. "It must be an interesting place."

"It was once the center of a vast empire and therefore carries a wealth of history, much more than New York City."

I had read something even more fascinating about London. It had a stock market, the London Stock Exchange.

I said goodbye to Maria and went back to my apartment. Then I ate a peanut butter and jelly sandwich and planned my trades for the following day.

The next morning, I went through my routine of visiting the NYSE and then decided to go to Lehman Brothers rather than call them because I saw great movements coming up in the markets.

After meeting my stockbroker and communicating my trades, he commented, "Your portfolio is doing very well, but have you thought any more about the risk being taken?"

"Not really," I replied.

"I'd highly advise you to diversify."

"I can do that," I stated.

"That's good. Although, there's one other thing. Have you filed your taxes?"

"Taxes?"

"You should be filing yearly taxes for your company, Tumbling Oak. With all the capital gains you have been making, the government would be very interested in your account."

"Capital gains? What's that?"

"Just that. If there is a profit when you sell, you owe taxes."

"And how much is that?"

"Around sixty percent."

I quickly approximated the amount I would have to pay, and an image of the oak tree projected into the space in front of me. A buzzard sat on one of the limbs, and it was the tax people. The entire tree was shriveling and dying as though taxes were stopping the flow of water to its roots.

The tax people were run by the government, and they would take away most of what I was earning. Then I recollected what Louie had said about what the government had done in Iwo Jima and how the government was worse than the Mafia. Suddenly the oak tree became dark, the same kind of darkness as when I met the policeman at Mario's bucket shop office in Chicago.

I asked, "Did the government come to you?

"No, why?"

"I'd like to move the Tumbling Oak account."

"Why?"

"Does Lehman Brothers have an office in London?"

"Yes, we do."

"Can you open an account for me in London and transfer all my money over there?

"I don't understand."

I didn't know what to do. This man was supposed to be working for me. I tightened my cheeks and squeezed my eyes and gave him Al's intimidating look. "Do it," I commanded, trying to copy Al's voice.

My stockbroker looked at me, stayed frozen for a moment and then said, "Yes sir, Mr. Harkin."

* * *

After leaving Lehman Brothers, I immediately went to a trav agency and made arrangements, and then went to Mari apartment and knocked on the door.

She opened it and exclaimed, "Arlo, I'm happy to see you."

Rather than avoiding her eyes, I looked directly at he said, "Would you like to go to London?"

"To London?"

"It's what you said yesterday, that you want to visit it."

"Well of course. Maybe someday."

"What about today?"

"What?"

"Please get packed. We are on a Pan Am flight to London this evening." At the travel agency, I had booked two first-class tickets.

"Really?"

"Please get packed. It's urgent."

There was a dark, turbulent wave mounting up behind me, and a black river shot out in front of me, exactly like the black river that took me through the hallway and down the stairwell at Mario's office building in Chicago. This new river flowed to the airport and then to London, and I was compelled to follow it.

I went back to our apartment and packed and then it took time to find my passport. Louie had gotten us passports to go on a holiday in Cuba, but there was some kind of revolution trouble down there that stopped our trip.

Once I found my passport I left our apartment and carried my small suitcase to Maria's place.

Then we got a taxi and headed to the airport.

CHAPTER 20

was turbulent, London was even more so. The city
ttled, especially the cars and buses coming from
tion. To cross the street, one had to first look
rather than the other way around. This went
patterns of behavior, and I needed Maria
left the hotel.

to an area of the city called the Financial
e many investment companies were
on Stock Exchange. Lehman Brothers

I felt queasy for a few days when we got to London, wanting to sleep during the day and stay awake at night. Maria called it jetlag. There was a five-hour time difference between London and New York.

She didn't seem to suffer from this, so sometimes she left the hotel to go see her old friends. That was all right with me.

Knowing I had an appointment with a manager at Lehman Brothers, Maria took me to a place called Saville Row. It was a street full of clothing shops. In most of the stores, they took your measurements and then made the suit. But one store had already made suits hanging on racks.

We picked out one that was just slightly too big for me, but Maria said I would soon out-grow it. Then we picked out another one in a different color.

On a Monday morning when I walked with Maria to Lehman Brothers I looked at the window of a shop and saw our reflection. I thought we looked elegant together. I had never had a suit before, and my image in the window was surrounded by whirling metal grays.

At the Lehman Brothers office, Maria waited for me in a reception area when I went in to see the manager. He was tall and thin, and when he shook my hand, I realized I was taller than him.

He introduced himself as James Parker and invited me into a small conference room where we sat on comfortable padded chairs. There was a polished wooden table between us. On the wall were paintings of hunting dogs jumping over forest green hedges.

He said, "Mr. Harris from our office in New York informed me that you are transferring your funds to London. Are you moving here?" He spoke with a British accent, although in my few days in London I realized there were different kinds of British accents.

"I'm not sure I'm moving here," I replied.

"Then, may I ask why you are moving your funds?"

I wasn't sure what to say. Was it because Louie stated that the government was a buzzard worse than the Mafia or was it because of the black river? I replied, "I'm thinking to invest internationally."

"Oh, I see," Mr. Parker said. "From our point of view, the United States is the best place in the world to invest. The economy is thriving."

"That's true, but don't you think there are other places to invest."

"For sure. I don't want to question your decision, but that seems a bold initiative to move your funds to the United Kingdom. Have you considered the tax situation here?"

"What do you mean?"

"We currently have a government in place that applies heavy taxes."

"More than sixty percent?" I asked.

"Oh yes."

I saw clouds darker than the darkest black. Had I made a wrong decision in following the dark river to London? "Would you have any solutions?" I asked.

Parker nodded. "We have experts who can assist in this sort of thing."

Mr. Parker arranged a meeting with accountants and specialists who recommended what they called, "international structures" that allowed one to buy and sell stocks in all markets in the world.

We decided on setting up a new company called an 'off-shore,' but I had difficulty with the term. If a company was off of a shore, did that mean it was in the middle of the ocean? Louie would be proud. Then, I saw commotion when wondering something. What would buzzard Mafia governments do if they learned about the company.

* * *

Being in London was like heaven for Maria. She caught up with old friends, she went to musicals and stage plays, and she visited shops. I went to a musical comedy with her but found it overwhelming. The songs and dancing caused turbulence and sometimes during the show I needed to put my hands over my ears and shut my eyes. The laughter of the crowd was unsettling.

We ate together in fancy restaurants, but that too created turmoil.

Maria was sensitive to my reactions and did everything possible to help me. Eventually what I found most satisfying was to stay in my hotel room and have meals brought there.

One of the best things about London is that they had many different newspapers, both morning and afternoon editions. Each day I got all of them and read them from cover to cover. I also bought day-old copies of the New York Times and the Wall Street Journal.

This got me back on track with my investments and each day I visited Mr. Parker at Lehman Brothers and told him what to buy and sell on markets around the world.

After a month in London, I wondered what Louie was doing and called our apartment in New York. There wasn't an answer. So, I called the Hope Center in upstate New York, and after five minutes of waiting, Louie came to the phone.

"Arlo?" He asked. "Where have you been? I've tried to reach you at home every day and even went there over the weekend. Where are you?"

"London," I answered.

"What?"

"I'm okay. I came here with Maria."

"You mean that beatnik acting woman."

He had never met Maria and didn't realize how helpful she was. Beatnik was a word to look up in the dictionary. "She's my friend," I said.

"Did she convince you to go to London?"

"No. I decided on my own and then asked her to come with me."

"What for?"

"Because I saw black clouds in New York."

The line went quiet for a moment then Louie said, "I see. And what about London? Do you see black clouds?"

"Yes, but I found a light blue river and things are okay." Louie was the only person I could tell about my colors.

"When are you coming back?"

"I don't know. Maybe in a month or two."

"I hope so," He said. "I don't like you being so far away."

It was hard to understand that. What difference would it make if I was in New York or London? In fact, London seemed a preferable solution because I was away from Louie's Mafia government, although I still wasn't exactly sure what that was. Knowing he had been at the Hope Center for a month, as initially planned, I asked him, "When are you coming home?"

The line went quiet again, and when he spoke, I sensed he was searching for words. "Arlo, this place is beneficial for me. There are people to talk with, especially about what I experienced during the war and the effect it had on me. I think I still need to work on some personal stuff."

I remembered all the times in the middle of the night when I heard him screaming about Iwo Jima and other irrational things. "You mean they help you with your nightmares?"

"Yes, you could say that. And, there's another thing. This place really is a hope center. We talk about things that are beyond this world, yet an essential part of it."

"Like what?"

"Like God."

That I didn't understand, but if it helped Louie, then logically I should have a glad kind of feeling.

We talked some more, and I told him how I would like to see some of Europe. In the window of a travel agency, I had seen a poster of Paris and the Eiffel Tour, and another of the hills of Tuscany in Italy, and one with enormous snow-covered mountains in Switzerland. We decided that I would call him back in a week.

After we hung up, I went back to reading newspapers when I heard Maria's door open and shut. Her hotel room was next to mine. I went into the hallway and knocked on the door, and she opened it. She had been shopping for a purse, as I had given her money to buy one. She was always grateful when I gave her money, and now she had colorful clothing to wear.

I asked her, "How long are we allowed to stay in London?"

"What do you mean?"

"We were given tourist visas when we arrived. Do you know when they will put us in jail?"

She smiled. "Maybe that's something to consider."

"We should move on," I stated.

"Move on to where?"

"To Europe. In a travel agency, I saw posters. There are things to see. Is there any place you would like to visit?"

Maria scratched her chin and then her eyes slightly widened. "For years there has been one place I desired to see, but never thought it was possible."

"Where is it?"

"I'd like to visit my home village in Spain."

When she said that I saw the dark cloud emerge from her colors and it expanded behind her. The only way to describe it was like a black baseball mitt.

CHAPTER 21

The following day I went to Lehman Brothers, and Mr. Peters ordered five thousand dollars of American Express Traveler's Cheques for me.

He said, "It is remarkable what has been achieved since you first came here a month ago."

"It's been thirty-five days," I corrected.

With his glasses positioned at the end of his nose, he peered over them and grinned, "Yes, you are probably right." He paused. "What do you want to do during your trip around Europe?"

"What do you mean?"

"What if the markets crash? With the high risk you carry, all could be lost."

I didn't see it that way. "In two weeks from now, on Thursday I'd like you to sell all my long positions and then immediately go short. Keep that position until the following Tuesday and then put half into cash and the remaining half into long positions."

I told him the specific futures and stocks to invest in.

He took his glasses off his nose and shook his head. "Some would say those are highly risky trades. Are you sure that is what you want to do?"

"Yes, long, short and then half long." In traders' terms, long was only a way of saying you expected the stock to go up, whereas short meant you expected the stock to go down.

"You're the client." He paused again. "May I ask something?"

"Sure."

"You are thirteen years old."

"In four months I'll be fourteen," I corrected him.

"Okay, soon to be fourteen. I'm wondering if you have a guardian. What is a boy of your age, from New York, doing in

London on his own? Who is looking out for you?"

"I'm from California."

"But you were referred by our office in New York."

"I was living there in my apartment."

"Do you have a guardian?"

"My Uncle Louie."

"Would it be possible to speak with him?"

"I guess, but you would have to call him."

"And, where is he?"

"In Hope Center in upstate New York."

"New York?"

"Yes. Louie calls it an insane asylum."

Mr. Peters stopped like he didn't know what to say. Finally, he asked, "You mean you are here in London on your own?"

"Maria is with me," I stated.

"Maria? Who is Maria?"

"She's my friend who did movies with David Niven and had a heart murmur, and feeds pigeons in Central Park. Louie calls her a beatnik."

Mr. Peters didn't ask any more questions.

* * *

The following day Maria and I took a train from London to Dover where we got on a boat and crossed the English Channel. Maria called it La Manche, for that is what the French called the channel.

Then, we got on a train to Paris that went through a picturesque countryside of farms and forests. The fields and orchards emanated with golden yellows and light greens, the kind of green you get in late winter and early spring. Sometimes my flowing rivers were that kind of green.

The clacking and movement of the train had a calming effect on me. Here I didn't experience the turbulence that extruded from New York, Chicago, and London.

As I turned from gazing out the window, I noticed that Maria was watching me. Finally, she said, "Arlo, you have made considerable progress in your acting."

"You mean acting normal?" I grinned as she had taught me.

"Yes, in acting normal. With a bit more practice, I'm not sure you'll need me anymore. But, if you are not feeling feelings, in the traditional sense of feelings, then you should be aware that you may not always get your expressions right. In that case, it is best to downplay your expressions rather than being too overt."

"You mean like this?" I gave her my Al look with the tight face."

"Exactly. Don't overdo it."

"Okay."

She hesitated a moment then stated, "I'm baffled what it's like not to have feelings. It is something so natural for me, probably coming from my Latin origins."

"I've always been this way."

"You are such a complex yet fascinating young man. May I ask another question?"

"Sure."

"Without prying, may I ask what you were doing at Lehman Brothers?"

"I trade stocks."

Her eyes opened wide. "What? You are only thirteen years old. How do you do it?"

"I'm almost fourteen."

"But, how do you do it?"

"I tell them what to buy and sell."

"That's not what I meant. How do you know what to buy and sell?"

I looked her in the eyes because that's what you do when you get serious with someone. "I see results before they happen."

"What?"

"Yes. I see if stocks are going to go up or down, and then I invest."

"You predict the future?"

"Yes and no. If there are numbers involved, like with horse races and the stock markets, then I see patterns."

"What about other things?"

"Not so much, but sometimes I see images having nothing to do with numbers, for instance, colorful rivers that lead me to places. And occasionally, I can predict events before they happen."

Maria laughed. "Maybe you are like Nostradamus."

"Who is that?"

"A man who lived in the Middle-Ages and some say he was a prophet. He saw the end of the world. But, there were other prophets like in the Old Testament in the Holy Bible and John who lived on the island of Patmos in Greece. He wrote the last book of the Bible."

I said, "I can't see the end of the world."

"Well, maybe you are not Nostradamus, but you may want to explore this gift. You never know."

"I don't need to know that," I said. "I just want to use my abilities to think and grow rich."

"Arlo, it sounds like you are already rich. Why do you need more?"

"Because there's nothing else I could do."

Maria smiled. "There are many other things you could do."

"Like what?"

"Maybe use your wealth to help poor people. Or, use it for scientific research. That's just a start, but there are many other things."

"I'll think about it," I said.

Her comments were curious. The logic as I saw it was that to help poor people, it meant you needed to have that particular feeling called empathy. That was an emotion experienced deep inside. Maybe I could learn it like I was learning body language, but I had doubts.

Scientific research was something different, but here again, the logic was complex. In thinking of this, confusing colors swirled around me and made me dizzy. While some people might use their wealth for scientific research, how would one know what research to give to?

The act of giving to poor people or scientific research involved value judgments. Those were too complex for me.

My goal was more comfortable, to just think and grow rich. The routines involved with this could merely be enacted day after day, by making decisions based on rhythmic flows of cause and effect, extrapolating forces and numbers and colors, while balancing relationships between a myriad of variables.

No, I would stay away from complex value judgments for even the thought of it made me wobble.

CHAPTER 22

The train pulled into the Paris Gare du Nord train station, and we took down our bags from the overhead racks above our seats. I wore a suit, and my small suitcase was stuffed with the second suit we had bought in London.

Immediately when stepping off the train, I was overwhelmed by the masses of people walking on the platform, and my reaction was to flee to the countryside.

We hired a porter who took our bags to a taxi and Maria spoke French and jabbered something to the driver.

The taxi driver drove fast, first through the countryside from the airport to the city, and then through the tangle of little streets where it seemed like the small cars were fighting each other. Horns honked, and drivers yelled at each other.

Before we left London, Maria had made reservations for us in Paris, at a medium-priced hotel which she said was on the Left Bank. I wondered what kind of bank that was until she explained that it was on the left side of the Seine River.

At times, I hunkered down in the backseat of the taxi and covered my eyes to avoid the mayhem. But, I was also thinking about Nostradamus and this John from Patmos that Maria had mentioned. Who were these people? I was curious to find out more.

We spent a week in Paris, and Maria always stayed with me when we went outside. Our hotel was in the Latin Quarter, which was full of small shops and coffee bars with tables on the sidewalks. It was often difficult to find a place to sit.

We took short walks in the mornings and afternoons, and Maria avoided the busy streets, although one time we went to a big boulevard called the Champs Elysees. The French people didn't say it like you see it spelled.

At the top of a long grade, the Champs Elysees led to a monument called the Arch de Triumph. That was where they had military parades and honored the grave of someone named The Unknown Soldier. I indeed wished Uncle Louie could see this, but maybe he had enough of war.

Maria also took me to art galleries. The biggest was The Louvre, a gigantic palace on the banks of the Seine River. I wanted to spend hours in there, for the colors of the paintings brought spectacular formations I had never seen before. There, I focused on minute details in the art and pointed out colors and shapes that Maria didn't notice.

On our seventh day in Paris, on a Sunday, Maria took me to a large old church called Notre Dame, which means 'our lady.' A church service was in progress and organ music was playing. Toward the front of the church, there were significant colorful windows, and they pulled me forward like magnets.

At the front of the church, the leaders wore white robes and swung large silver balls on silver chains. Sweet smelling smoke came from the balls. I went to the front, walked up a few steps and went past the men in robes. Two young boys wearing white robes stood next to the men. The boys held candlesticks with lighted candles.

A hush went over the crowd, and the men at the front stopped what they were doing. The boys giggled, like the kids at the swimming pool back in California.

I continued and then stood below the round glass windows. The colors from the windows swooped down and overwhelmed me, and it was like my inner being left me, and ethereal beings lifted me upward.

One of the men in a robe said, "*C'est interdit d'aller la bas.*"

Then I heard Maria's voice. "Arlo, you can't go there. This is their church service, and this area is forbidden to the public."

The colors of the windows twirled in my head. "But why?" I asked.

"Just because, because that is a place where only the priests can go."

"But why? The colors swirling from the glass window are amazing. I'm standing in the best place."

She looked up at the stained-glass windows and nodded, and then turned to the head priest and said, "*Excusez-nous mon père, mais il est spécial.*"

The priest peered down at me, and I couldn't read his look. Maybe it was an expression used in France. It seemed he was attempting to convey authority. So, I gave him the biggest smile I could make. He didn't change his facial expression. Then I switched to my best Al look, face tight, eyebrows jutting forward.

The priest took a step back, and the two boys holding the candles started to laugh out loud.

"*Partez s'il vous plaît.*" the priest commanded, waving his hand toward the front doors of the church.

Maria took my hand, and we walked down the long corridor in the middle of the church, and people stared at us. Some were smiling, even giggling, and the noise of their talking grew louder.

As we got to the back of Notre Dame the organ began to play, and when we stepped outside, I said to Maria, "The windows did something to me."

"Yes, I could see that," she said. "What was it?"

"I don't know for sure, but something is going to happen. It was like someone being lifted upward."

"Arlo, you are very different, but I like it. You are like a precious son." She went up on her tiptoes, pulled me down by the neck and kissed me on the forehead.

Maria's kiss triggered new images that I hadn't seen before. Her lips were soft, and I felt her breath when she moved away from me. When I looked carefully at her lips, they had small wrinkles around them. Her hands were also wrinkled. Some might call her imperfect because of her age, but it was remarkable that such tenderness could be expressed by someone.

Pink colors emanated from her. At the park, I had seen mothers kiss their children like that, and it evoked reactions from the children. But, I didn't feel anything, only experiencing colors.

"Thank you," I said.

"For what?" She asked.

"For the kiss. I was wondering what it would feel like."

"You mean you've never been kissed, by your mother or grandmother?"

"Not that I can remember."

"Oh my, I don't know what to say."

"There is nothing to say," I stated. "But, you gave me many things to think about."

"Like what?"

"So many things, like learning to look at body language, the paintings at The Louvre, looking at expressions of people, and happiness and sadness and tenderness. And, you mentioned Nostradamus and this John from Patmos in Greece, which are new things to consider."

"Arlo, I've also learned things from you, and I'm immensely grateful for the heart operation and for saving my life. That was an incredible act of kindness."

It had more to do with logic, but when she mentioned saving her life, I had a recurrence of the image I had seen in the church, of floating upwards.

* * *

In the afternoon of the following day, Maria came to my hotel room carrying a brown paper bag. She had a sizeable happy kind of smile on her face and said, "I have something for you."

These were the moments where I saw conflicting colors. On my birthday and at Christmas my grandfather had always given me gifts, mainly toy farm machinery like tractors and trucks and plastic animals. On those occasions, I had seen those clashing colors and my body shook, for this was outside the usual pattern.

I looked at Maria's bag and hoped my body would not shake. "Shall we wait for Christmas?" I asked.

She laughed. "Of course not." She reached into her bag, pulled out two books, and handed them to me. "It took me all morning to find these in English," she said.

The first one was bound in thick yellow paper, like many books I had seen in the outside bookstalls along the Seine River.

It was titled The Prophecies.

Maria said, "Remember I mentioned Nostradamus? That is a book written by him. People say he prophesied the future."

I turned it over, from front to back, and realized I missed reading. Then I held the second book. It was leather bound, thick but small. I looked inside, and the print was incredibly tiny, but readable.

"That is the *Sagrada Biblia*, the Holy Bible," she said. "Both books contain what I told you about, people who could predict what was going to happen. They call them *prophets*. I thought you might be interested to read about them, especially John who wrote the last book of the *Sagrada Biblia*."

"Thank you," I said. Maria had taught me to say that whenever people did things for you, like with waiters in restaurants and when the man gave your train tickets.

Indeed, I was interested because maybe I might learn something from these prophets. I stuffed the books in my suitcase and had difficulty in closing it.

CHAPTER 23

The following morning, we took a train south through France and stopped in Lyon where we ate some tasty chicken and spent the night. French food produced more subtle flavors than in America or London, making sophisticated colors that filled your mouth and the room.

The following day we rode the train to the south of France and Maria slept much of the time. I figured that our week in Paris had worn her out. As I watched the countryside passing by the train, there were fascinating colors. The fields and small towns blended into a light blue river with green and black streams joining in. It seemed our voyage was on the accurate path.

The train stopped in towns named Nimes and Montpellier.

To the south was Spain, and I was most curious to see the village where Maria came from before her family moved to the United States. She said she still had cousins there and that she had kept up with them over the years. But, this was her first time back since childhood.

Maria woke up when the train got to Perpignan, not far from the border with Spain.

"Who was this Nostradamus," I asked her.

"I believe he lived in a small village near Marseille, to the east of us."

"I'd like to find out more about him and to visit where he lived. Can we do this after we visit your village?"

Maria laughed. "Arlo, you are paying for this trip. Your desires should come first."

"Then after your village, let's go find out about him."

She nodded and went back to sleep.

The thought of Nostradamus fascinated me. It was something new to discover, very different than horse racing and stock markets. My most basic question was whether I was like Nostradamus, as Maria suggested. And I wanted to learn more about the other prophets Maria mentioned, especially this John from Patmos in Greece.

Maybe there were other people like me?

We changed trains at the border between France and Spain. The rails were wider in Spain, so the trains couldn't go from one country to the other. We also went through the French and Spanish customs.

The Spanish customs officers were called *La Guardia Civile*, stern-faced men who carried guns at their sides and wore shiny hats, round in the front and flat and turned up on the back.

One of the officers held up my passport and then held Maria's next to mine. He babbled something in Spanish and Maria responded, and I gave him my biggest smile followed by Al's smile. That seemed to be working these days.

Another officer began to laugh, so our passports were handed back to us.

When we got on the train, Maria said, "You almost gave me a heart attack."

"Why is that?"

"You should not make fun of the Guardia Civile. These are hard men who work for the general who rules Spain. Always be serious around them."

"I liked their hats."

"You mean, the *sombrero de tres picos*?"

"Is that what you call it?" I asked.

"Yes. It is also called the *tricornio*. Do not make fun of these men. We could get into trouble."

As the train headed south, I reflected on what Maria said. Why would these men be so hard and why would people need to be careful when around them?

The train was less comfortable in Spain, hard wooden seats and bumpy tracks. Three hours after leaving the border we checked into a hotel in Barcelona near a street called La Rambla.

In the evening, we went out and had tapas, small dishes with olives, sliced ham, fried potatoes and octopus and things from the sea that were new to me.

As Maria began to eat the tapas, tears come from her eyes.

"Are you okay," I asked?

"More than you can imagine," she replied.

"Why does that food make you cry?"

She smiled and took a paper napkin and wiped a tear from her cheek. "It's not just the food. It's everything, the food, the warm weather, families walking down La Rambla, everything. I have waited a lifetime to experience this."

"Why is that?"

"After my family left Spain, there was a civil war here. We never came back, and I didn't even come back here when I was living in London before World War II. Spain was a tense place, and it still is."

"Why is that?"

"Did you see the Guardia Civile at the border?"

"The men with the shiny pointy hats?"

"Yes. They work for the man who runs the country." She changed the tone of her voice and whispered, "General Franco. He is a dictator and people are not free to express themselves like we do in the United States."

"Even now?" I asked.

"Yes, even now. So, I'd ask you to be very careful and don't go to the front of churches when Mass is taking place, and don't talk back to anyone in authority. The authorities can be very harsh. Do you understand that?

"I think so," I said. This was the second time she gave that warning, and I saw something dark forming on the horizon.

"Good. Now, let's enjoy the evening."

The tapas were tasty, not as color-evoking as French cooking, but the subdued evening was harmonious and peaceful. I watched the people strolling along La Rambla, and it didn't have the same impact as other big cities. What was different was that they didn't seem to be in a hurry and that gave soft images, not like the turbulent colors of Paris and London.

The following morning, we took a taxi to the Barcelona Sants train station, which is the central train station in Barcelona. There, I exchanged some American Express traveler's cheques from dollars into Pesetas. Then we headed east in the direction of Madrid.

The train ran slower than in France, and the rail cars were older with hard wooden seats. Going west, we traveled inland, and an hour and a half after leaving Barcelona the train stopped at a place that seemed in the middle of nowhere, a town called Lleida.

"Is this your village?" I asked.

"No. We have to go to Sudanell which is twenty minutes away."

We took a taxi, and in the distance on a hill, I saw a small village. Maria was crying.

"Why do you cry?" I asked. That was the second time in less than twenty-four hours that I asked her that question.

"Arlo, you don't know what this means to me. To be home."

To be honest, I didn't know what that meant, for it was a feeling that was foreign to me. I responded in the way she had taught me. "Yes, I think I understand."

She looked at me and narrowed her eyes. "You are a good student, but you don't fool me."

That told me that I needed to work more on my body language and verbal responses.

The taxi drove into a large open area in the middle of the village. The church was at one end and shops were around the edges. Several large trees gave shade to benches where some old men sat and talked.

After we paid the taxi, Maria immediately headed toward a side street. I carried my small suitcase and her large one. She stopped in front of a door and knocked, and a minute later the door opened. A woman appeared who seemed to be the same age as Maria, and Maria said, *"Consuela, Esta mi, Maria."*

The woman had long silver hair that flowed down her back, and she wore a cotton dress with a cotton apron. She raised her hands and screamed something and then the two of them hugged and then stepped away from each other while still holding hands and they began to ramble away in Spanish.

After that, I was introduced, and this was followed by several more minutes of machine gun Spanish with both women rapidly talking at the same time. Then, Consuela led us to a couple of rooms. My room was simple with a single bed and lumpy mattress. There was an old wooden table against one wall and wooden chair that moved and squeaked when you sat on it.

There were no paintings on the wall, only a cross with a man hanging on it, his arms stretched out to the side. It looked like some pins or nails went through his hands and his feet. I had seen something similar at the Notre Dame Cathedral, only a hundred times bigger. And, there were many paintings in the Louvre with this image, that viewed the man on the cross from different angles. I would ask Maria about this. Why was he so important?

At ten in the evening, we ate, which was the usual time for dinner in Spain and then I went to bed.

In the morning, we had coffee with milk, which Maria called *Café con Leche,* along with bread and sliced meat and cheese. The simplicity of it extruded a harmonious blend of pinks and blues.

After breakfast, Maria and I went with Consuela to the village square, and before you knew it, there was a small crowd around Maria. People laughed and cried and hugged her, and somehow that triggered the memory of Maria's kiss, as though there was a connected association.

I used this as an opportunity to slip away, for on one side of the village I saw what looked to be an orange grove. But, in getting closer, it was a lemon grove. Even so, it resurrected images of our place in California. The citrus grove and the Spanish spoken in the village somehow reminded me of Carlos, and for the first time, I wondered how he was doing.

This triggered off something in my inner being, which caused me to walk from one end of the lemon grove to the other. The sun filtered through the leaves, and just like in California, the colors were almost musical, light yellows and blues, although there was a metallic purple stream that raced ahead of all the other colors.

Just beyond the lemon grove was a group of shrubby oak trees, much smaller than our oak tree back home. I avoided touching those trees, remembering the electrical shock from our oak tree.

After walking back and forth several times through the lemon grove, I had a revelation. Now I understood why we had come here, for the menacing dark mitt made sense.

CHAPTER 24

The village was small, six hundred and fifty-three people and it seemed like everyone was related in some distant way to everyone else. Besides Maria, there was only one other person who spoke English, but I didn't mind. Their unintelligible words formed colorful streams, first from one person and then another. Then the hues of their words merged into rivers, bending and flowing, and that gave me a sense of their conversations.

Maria apologized to me for many things, for staying so long, that no one spoke English, and for the modest living conditions and simple meals. I told her that we could stay as long as needed. The village and surrounding were harmonious. My daily routine was to walk in the lemon orchard which was soothing compared to the attacking turmoil of London and New York.

Maria spent much of her time in the village square sitting on benches talking with the villagers. The conversations were animated, everyone speaking with loud guttural voices. Young children played tag and kicked balls. Workers came and went, often stopping for five or ten minutes to get involved in the topics discussed.

Every day Maria went to the village church to light a candle and pray. I went with her several times and was fascinated by the statues and paintings inside. Like Notre Dame in Paris, it had stained glass windows except they were much smaller and not as ornate.

In the front of the church was a sizeable statue of the man hanging on the cross. I spent considerable time looking at the details, the ring of thorns resting on his head, how they punctured his forehead. His head tilted to one side, and the countenance on his face was sorrow. Maria had taught me that expression.

He was undressed except for a small cloth. Large nails went through his hands and feet, and there was a wound on his side. From this, I sensed great pain, and I saw the blood flowing from those injuries, and they became a red river that enlarged itself like the Mississippi River, and it went across the lands, and it brought a mystery, which I wanted to learn more about.

One day as Maria was praying I asked her, "Who is this man?"

She sat at the end of the long bench in the second row her head covered with a scarf, hands folded, and eyes closed. She opened her eyes and asked, "What man?"

"The man up there." I pointed to the man with the nails in his hands.

"It is Jesus."

"You mean Jesus Christ? I read about him in the Sunday edition of the New York Times, an article, *Was Jesus Really God.* There were several pages of commentary from different philosophers and religious people."

"Yes, that's Jesus there."

"Who was he?"

"Our savior and lord."

"What does that mean?"

She stood up and breathed heavy. She walked up to the statue and said, "We need to be saved from our sins. He died so that we might live."

"I don't understand sins," I said.

She smiled, looked at the statue and then at me and asked, "You don't understand sins?"

"Not really. I've seen the word in the newspapers but don't know what it is."

"In the church, sin is often viewed as breaking God's law or not following one of the rules of the church. But sin is more than that. It is a failure to live up to God's holy perfection."

That was a profound thought which I didn't fully grasp, but one question came to me. "Who is perfect?" I asked.

Maria smiled again, a smile that could never be forgotten. "Arlo, now you are on to something. No one is perfect, and therefore all have sinned, and all need the savior."

"Does that have anything to do with him hanging up there?"

"Yes, everything. You and I should be there and not him. He took our place. That's why he is called our Savior."

This was all new and strange, but there was logic. "Why is he still on the cross? They should put him in a grave like my grandfather."

Her eyes looked tired, and she said, "Why don't we talk about this later? I'd like to finish my prayers.

I saw she had tranquility. The church was dark, the only light coming from the narrow windows and from a few candles burning in front of a small painting of a woman. Yet, I saw a glow in Maria, and at that moment it confirmed my understanding of why the green river had led us here.

I walked from the church out into the bright sunshine. It was a warm day, and I went to the village square and sat on a bench in the shade. One young man came over to me. His name was Enrique, and he lived and worked in Barcelona, but came back to his village on weekends.

His English was broken, and I sensed he wanted to practice it, so he asked me questions about America.

I waited and waited for Maria, maybe an hour or so, and she didn't come out of the church, and I knew it was time. So, I went inside the church where it took a while for my eyes to adjust to the darkness.

She was on the floor, motionless. I approached her knowing she had died, a white eminence surrounding her, like I had seen on my grandfather when he lay beneath the orange tree.

I knew this was coming. It was our purpose in being here. Maria's black mitt had been getting more prominent over the past days, and this was the outcome.

In guessing horses, I needed momentum with numbers to determine results but guessing this was very different. Maybe in some small way, I had this prophecy ability that Maria talked about.

I stood and watched her for a while, seeing tranquility in the translucent fog that surrounded her, then there was an invisible rising like I had experienced in front of the stained-glass windows of Notre Dame.

Walking outside I went over to Enrique who was talking to one of the girls from the village. It seemed they especially liked each other, for they didn't notice when I approached them.

I tapped Enrique on the shoulder and said, "Maria died."

He looked at me with a lip turned up, one eye squinting and asked, "*Por favor*?"

"Maria died. She had a wounded heart, and she is in the church."

He made me repeat what I said, that she had a wounded heart and died in the church. Then he said something to the girl, and they ran into the church, and a few moments later he ran out of the church and called to the women who were in the village square.

Seven or eight women hurried into the church, and a few moments later I heard a kind of screaming or wailing, women being overtaken by emotion.

Two of the women came out and ran over to a building. Maria had told me it was the office of the village mayor, but he was rarely there, spending most of his time working in the fields. Then one of the women went to a small house beside the church, and a man came out dressed in a long black robe with a large cross hanging around his neck. He scampered toward the church with the two women trailing behind.

Then the frenzy increased. One person told another, and people began to appear on side streets, and before you knew it, over one hundred people went into the church. This was followed by crescendos of wailing and the loud noise of villagers talking.

I was fascinated by the activity, and it reminded me of an ant's nest poked with a stick.

It was pleasant on the bench with the shade of the tree and a small breeze blowing. It reminded me of warm summer days in California, yet the turmoil going on in the church conflicted with the mood of the day, so I walked down to the lemon grove and paced from one end to the other.

When I got back to the village, I saw that people had long sad faces, some women with red eyes. It is hard to tell if some were truly sad, or if that was the body language they were trained to do in these circumstances.

They left Maria in the church, as there was no other place to put her. Eventually, two men showed up with a wooden coffin.

Then Enrique came to me, along with the priest and another man who was dressed in dusty blue pants and a sweat-stained long sleeve shirt. He wore a blue beret, his shoes were dirty, and he carried a garden hoe. Enrique explained that he was the mayor and they wanted to ask me some questions.

Enrique translated.

The priest asked, "You told Enrique that Maria had heart problems. How do you know this?"

"I paid for her heart operation in New York. They were able to fix some of her heart but not all of it."

"How old are you," asked the mayor.

"I'm thirteen."

The priest and mayor looked at each other, and then the mayor asked. "It must have been an expensive operation. How did you pay for it?"

"I used to make money on the horse races, but now I invest in the stock market."

They had a discussion that lasted quite a while which seemed more like an argument. Finally, Enrique said, "They don't believe that a thirteen-year-old boy could make money on the stock market. Of course, they hardly know what that is."

"Tell them I am almost fourteen."

Enrique translated that, and there was another lengthy discussion. Then the priest asked, "How did you meet Maria?"

"She was on a park bench feeding pigeons."

Enrique didn't translate but questioned me, "Feeding pigeons?"

"Yes. She was also feeding sparrows that were competing with the pigeons for food. You should tell them that."

Enrique hesitated and then said something in Spanish.

I was uncertain what their facial expressions and body language meant. They became quiet, and the mayor tilted his head and looked at the priest while raising his palms in the air. The priest shook his head back and forth, quick jerky movements. Maybe Enrique wasn't doing a correct job of translating.

The mayor asked, "How did you get to Spain with Maria?"

"By train, but first by boat across the English Channel and of course by airplane from New York to London."

Enrique said, "That's not what he meant. Why were you and Maria traveling together? Where are your parents? Who was Maria to you?"

"My father is dead, and my mother is in San Diego in California, but I haven't seen her for seven years or more. And Maria taught me acting?"

"Acting," Enrique asked.

"Yes, about body language and how to be normal."

Enrique looked at me and said, "I'm not sure how to translate all that."

They gabbled on in Spanish, and then the priest asked, "Were you there when Maria died?"

"No, I was sitting here on the bench."

"But, you knew she had a weak heart."

"Yes, I knew she was going to die."

Enrique translated, and the three of them looked at each other in silence. "How did you know that?" Enrique asked.

"Because, I had seen darkness behind her, like a baseball mitt. It had been getting bigger and more menacing."

"Menacing? What is that word?" Enrique asked.

"It means something like dangerous or angry like it wants to hurt you."

"And you saw this?

"Yes, I see it sometimes in people. A few people here in the village have it."

Enrique froze. "You mean you know what people in our village are going to die?"

"Yes. Before coming here, I wasn't exactly sure what the mitt was, but now I do. We were led here by the green river, so Maria could die in happiness in her own village. These were good days for her."

Enrique translated, and the priest and mayor stiffened and moved back from me. A lengthy discussion occurred, and my attention drifted off to the lemon grove. I wondered if we could plant some lemons on our property in California.

The priest asked, "By what powers do you perform these signs?"

"What do you mean?"

"By what divine powers do you see these death signs? Is it from good or evil?"

Again, I didn't understand what he meant. "I simply saw them in the Church when she was praying after we talked about sin and the savior."

After Enrique translated, the priest took a deep breath, and he smiled. "*Esta bueno,*" he said.

I understood that because it was a term Carlos used. I said, "I'd like to leave some money to pay for Maria's funeral, to pay for the casket and any expenses, but especially that she should have a beautiful tombstone." I reached into my pocket and took out a wad of Pesetas that was worth around five hundred dollars and handed it to the priest. "Is it enough?"

Enrique answered. "Much more than enough. We can build a house for that."

"Just a beautiful tombstone," I said. "And if there's anything left over please give it to poor people in the village. I'm not sure why, but Maria said one should do that with money."

The priest smiled and said, "*Muchas gracias.*"

There was silence, and the mayor said, "Maria has a bruise on her temple. It seems she slipped forward from her praying position and hit the bench in front of her. But, we are afraid it could be interpreted differently."

When Enrique translated that it made me curious. "What does he mean?"

Enrique looked to the right and left, as though no one should listen to what he said. In fact, many people stood across from us in small groups in the village square. They had been quietly watching the entire discussion. He whispered, "The authorities, the Guardia Civil will come from Lleida. You were the last to see Maria alive, and we think it is best if you leave here."

"I don't understand."

"With the Guardia Civil, they always look for someone guilty. You are, even if you are not. They will see the hurt on Maria's head and then ask questions and make blame."

"You mean they would think I killed her?"

He nodded. You come with me to Barcelona, and we must fast leave. Someone from the village will drive us to Lleida, and then we take the train to Barcelona.

I quickly went to my room, packed my suitcase and a few minutes later we were in an old car speeding down a dusty road. I turned around and saw Sudanell, Maria's village, and a white shroud covered it, and my logic told me we had done the proper thing in coming here, for she had found peace.

But, an army-green mist rose up behind the shroud. It was the color of the Guardia Civil and their boss, the Dictator. It wanted to suffocate the village and everything around it.

CHAPTER 25

On the train to Barcelona, Enrique sat stiffly on the wooden seat, and each time the train stopped at a village he bent over by the window and looked at the people on the platform.

He said, "We must think that the people in Sudanell will not say anything because they do not like the Guardia Civil. But one never knows. The Guardia Civil makes threats. They will seek a guilty person for Maria's death. If they hear a strange story about a young Americano being with Maria when she died, they will look for you."

"But, I didn't do anything."

He nodded. "That doesn't matter. They will make truth into anything they want. They are not trusting, and your story about horse racing and feeding pigeons and acting lessons is not easy to, ah, *creer*... to believe."

The same black river emerged, the one when I met the policemen at Mario's bucket shop in Chicago. It swept alongside the train and flowed through Barcelona and went eastward.

"Enrique, I don't think I should take the train out of Spain because the Guardia Civil is at the border. Is there another way? I need to go east."

"East? To where?"

"Perhaps to Marseille in France." The village of Nostradamus was close by Marseille.

He remained silent like he was trying to think of a solution. As I waited, the continual clacking of the train's wheels filled me with a new sensation, which could only be described as momentum. It was very different than the currents I saw with numbers like it had more to do with history than financial outcomes. The black mitt was only a part of this.

Finally, Enrique said, "I have friend who works on docks in Barcelona. On the Mediterranean, some cargo boats take people. We maybe find you a boat."

* * *

In Barcelona, Enrique lived in a room he rented from a family, and there was no space for me, so I stayed at a small hotel with a basic room. It cost two dollars a night. I liked it better than the hotel in Paris, for everything in the place was minimalized, like my bedroom at our home in California and like the simple room at Maria's cousin's house.

I ventured out into the streets of Barcelona to get food and found a newsstand that sold a few out-of-date newspapers from England, so each day I'd go back to the hotel and read. Mostly they had articles about the queen and her family, movie stars and scandals, with little financial information.

Then I found the central post office in Barcelona where you could make international calls, so I called Mr. Peters at Lehman Brothers in London.

"Arlo," he said, "Your trades have been marvelous."

For two weeks, I had not looked at the stock market results, with one week in Paris and another week in Sudanell. "What are the results?"

"We traded exactly as you instructed. There have been enormous swings in the markets over the past two weeks, and your timing was impeccable. You doubled the value of your portfolio."

That meant I had over three hundred thousand dollars in my account. I said, "I'd now like to make some commodities trades." And I gave him instructions to buy positions on futures and options.

He was quiet for a moment and said, "These seem rather extreme. You are betting one hundred percent of your portfolio on things considered to be highly risky by most investors. You could lose everything."

As he spoke, I observed tides, rolling waves, like those seen at the CBOT in Chicago, only this time I wasn't watching floor-traders waving their hands in the air. "That's what I want to do," I stated.

There was more silence, and he finally said, "I will set up the trades immediately."

I told him I would call him again in two weeks and we ended the call.

Then I had a thought. Almost every time we spoke, he warned me about risk. This trade didn't seem risky, or was it? Perhaps yes, because this decision was made with very little real information.

Instead, I had been walking in a lemon grove for the past week, so on what basis had I made my choice? Suddenly, it was like the oak tree aimed shock waves at me all the way from California.

* * *

The thought of Mr. Peters warning me about risk, and of my sudden decision went through my mind over the following days. I wasn't interested in losing money, for this went against my goal to think and grow rich. But, that wasn't my main thought. It was more a question of where the image of the rolling waves had come from, the waves that informed me about making these trades? I had no answer.

Enrique visited me each day, and on the fifth day, he came to my room breathing heavily, droplets of sweat running down the sides of his face.

He said, "You must go now. A boat is leaving in one hour, and they will take you."

My clothing was already packed in my suitcase, so I picked it up, went downstairs and paid my hotel bill. Enrique led the way, and as we got to the front door of the hotel, he reached back and put his hand on my chest to stop me. He looked onto the street and then nodded his head, and we went outside.

"We must be cautious," he said. "The Guardia Civil are looking for you."

"What for?"

"They want to question you. It seems there was much discussion after you left the village. By saying you knew that Maria would die, it raised suspicion with the villagers, and there was much argument. Some said the source of your power was evil and others said it was good, like coming from God. This made the Guardia Civil very curious, and they are now looking for you. It is best you go."

"Why would the villagers say that about me, that my ability was of evil or good?"

"Because no one else sees dark... what did you call this thing? A mitt? No one else does this, so it is like you are an... *oráculo*."

"An oracle?"

"Yes, someone who tells fortunes. But an oracle person can be maybe good or maybe evil. This caused much fear."

"Why would they fear me?"

"You said you knew of Maria's death and there is another thing."

"What other thing?"

"You have a strange way."

"What do you mean?" I asked.

"You stare when you look and the way you walk in the lemon trees by the village. People watched you. The villagers say you are like a ghost or something from another world. The priest told this is not so, but they do not believe him so he will make a special Mass to purge the village of spirits."

Conflicting mixtures of colors flowed with his words as though they were at war with each other. I had never experienced anything like this before, except when kids at the swimming pool fought against each other. I knew I was different than others and did my best to act normal as Maria had taught me, but it wasn't working.

And this thought of good and evil was something new. In being honest with myself, I didn't really know the difference between good and bad, unless someone told me.

My grandfather had been categorical about certain things, and that gave me boundaries. Uncle Louie also had a lot of do's and don'ts, although he broke most of his own rules. And then Maria had said things that informed me about right and wrong.

Maybe there was wisdom here, for how can anyone know what is right or evil, without someone telling them? But, Enrique's concept of good and evil was a mystery, in speaking of ghosts and oracles.

Enrique led me through dark, narrow streets built hundreds of years before the United States of America was even a nation. The only illumination came from small windows on the apartments above street level.

The streets were cobblestone, and I had a difficult time to keep my footing. I stumbled several times and had to stop and put my hand on the dark stone walls. Then Enrique carried my suitcase, and I had better balance. I put my hand on his shoulder like I did with Louie.

We eventually came to the docks and went into an area where cargo boats were docked. After walking a long way, we arrived at a rusted boat with the name 'Christobol' barely legible on the back. It was smaller than the others, and we approached a gangplank that went from the dock to the vessel. It was narrow and swayed back and forth, and I hesitated, wondering if I would fall into the water.

Then I looked toward the end of the docks and saw two Guardia Civil officers walking in our direction. They were talking. A bolt of darkness fell from the sky, encircled them and then it spread like an ominous cloud in my direction.

I sprinted up the gangplank onto the top deck of the Christobol, meeting the overpowering smells of grease and diesel fumes.

Enrique led me to the room where the captain drove the ship, and he introduced me to Captain Pujols. Next to the captain was a crewman who looked at me with tight eyes that emitted a dark smoky atmosphere sending a warning. I equated that to Mario and Al and even Snodgrass and Minx, the two men at the racetrack.

The captain spoke a little English, and his words were yellow and green but broken like puffs breaking away from glue as he struggled to find words. He appeared less ominous than the crewman.

Then I gave Enrique the equivalent of fifty Dollars in Pesetas, and he handed it to Captain Pujols, who stuffed the money in his pocket and jabbered something in Spanish to Enrique.

I went with Enrique back to the top of the gangplank, gave him some money and said, "Thank you," as Maria had taught me.

Enrique shook my hand and said, "Be careful," and he left the boat and then disappeared between two buildings.

The gangplank was removed, and the engine rumbled, and the Christobol slowly left the docks, and I had no idea where we were going.

* * *

On the back of the boat with my small suitcase next to me, I sat on a coil of thick ropes and watched the lights of Barcelona disappear into the distance until finally, we were surrounded by darkness, except for a sliver of the moon and a sky filled with stars.

Then I considered that I was alone, a tall, almost fourteen-year-old boy by himself with a few strangers on a strange boat in a strange sea. Maybe I was the stranger?

Usually, I had familiar people in my sphere, like Louie and Maria, but this was very different.

And, something was perplexing. At that moment, I didn't see any significant streams or clouds or numbers, only a swirling, murky emptiness that filled the world.

That triggered a realization. While I didn't have a clue where the Christobol was going, it really didn't matter. More important than the destination of the boat, was the question of where I was going? Without the vision of a direction, it seems one is lost, even without hope.

In thinking deeply about it, I had two directions. First, there was the goal to think and grow rich, and it made sense. Because of my abilities, or rather because of my limitations, that is, my incapacity with social skills and in acting out proper body language, the think and grow rich objective was a logical choice. Goal number one was still valid.

But something else complicated my thinking. Maria had spoken of Nostradamus and of course those other prophets who were found in one of the books she gave me. She said I might be like them.

That thought stuck in my brain. Knowing I worked best when attempting on one task at a time, I decided that the think and grow rich goal needed to stand aside for a while. Maria's prophet question required an answer. Only how?

Then, another thought came to me, something more immediate. My stockbroker often warned me about risk, and I wondered if being on this boat was a risky situation, whatever that meant? One thing came to my mind, the cash and traveler's cheques in my suitcase. It would be difficult to successfully pursue Maria's prophet question if I lost that money. So, I opened the suitcase and put the cash and traveler's cheques in the pockets of my pants.

After several hours of thinking, the crew member with the hard eyes found me, and with a somber expression, he led me to a place to sleep. It was a small room with three thick hammocks, sagging sheets of canvas stretching from wall to wall, like bunk beds. Each had a well-worn blanket to cover yourself with.

The crewman signaled with his hand for me to take the top one. I put my suitcase on the floor, and he helped push me up on the hammock. I took off my pants, rolled them up, and used them as a pillow.

As the seaman left the room, I saw his eyes linger on my suitcase.

I was fatigued and immediately went to sleep, but during the night, there was shuffling in the room as crew members came and went.

I'm pretty good sleeper, so they didn't bother me too much except it was hot and stuffy up there. Being tired, I didn't really have the energy to think much more about my situation, although I did question if these sailors were like other people I met who stole your money, the buzzards.

When the morning light came through a round window in the room, I climbed down from my hammock and noticed my suitcase. A piece of my suit stuck through the opening. Someone had been in my suitcase and had closed it improperly.

I unrolled my pants, put them on, and then patted my front pockets. The cash and traveler's checks were still there. Looking again at the suitcase confirmed that I needed to take caution on this boat and anywhere else I went.

The seaman with the dark eyes entered the sleeping area and signaled for me to follow him. He glanced at the suitcase and then at the pockets of my pants, a bolt of blackish purple flowing from his eyes.

Then he led me to the galley, a narrow room with a long table and a small kitchen at one end. Breakfast consisted of pieces of white bread, which the French called *baguette*, with butter and jam. This was served with bowls of coffee, milk, and sugar. It was not the kind of breakfast that Louie made, but the simplicity of it gave me harmonious, soft blue colors.

An hour after breakfast, the cargo boat arrived in Palma de Mallorca, an island off the coast of Spain. I would have gotten off there to look around, but one of the crewmen, who spoke a little English, told me that Mallorca was part of Spain, and I still carried clear impressions of the Guardia Civil.

After the Christobol left Palma de Mallorca, I went to the steering cabin and asked Captain Pujols where we were going. There was a map of the Mediterranean stuck on the back wall, so he went to it and pointed with his finger. First, we would go to the islands of Sardinia and Corsica, and then Genoa, which was a port city on the North-West side of Italy.

The map caused me to wonder where I should go? Sometimes when I tried to make decisions, I only saw a confusing mix of colors, whereas, at others, streams and rivers flowed to a place.

Now, it was a confusing mix.

Should I go back to New York and be with Louie? Or, maybe go to London to visit Mr. Peters at Leeman Brothers? But, Maria's prophet question was primary, like a determined wind pushing me somewhere.

The two books from Maria were in my suitcase. She said that perhaps I was like the prophets in these books, so I was compelled to find out more.

Looking at the map, Genoa was not far from Marseille. Nostradamus had come from a nearby village. Perhaps that's where I should go? Yet, when I thought that, the complex mixes of colors still circled around me and at that point, I thought that maybe I should feel lost. Then, I wondered what it would be like to feel something like that.

CHAPTER 26

The Christobol made steady progress, and that gave me time to think. A bright blue sea stretched endlessly in every direction, and there were no significant distractions.

That allowed me to entirely focus on the first of Maria's books, The Prophecies, by Nostradamus.

When doing things, I get consumed by them, whether walking laps in the orange fields or reading the newspapers.

So, in two days I read the entirety of The Prophecies. It started with a Preface, which was really a fascinating letter from Nostradamus to his son. Would my father have written a letter like this?

Nostradamus told his son that the events described in his book have not yet come to pass, that all is governed by the power of Almighty God, and that his predictions were made through divine will and the spirit of prophecy.

Crimson fireworks appeared because this is what Maria described, someone who could see the future. It drew me toward Nostradamus because maybe he was like me.

The book consisted of ten centuries, which were more like chapters and each one contained many phrases of four lines each. They were four-line poems, but they didn't rhyme. In one I read,

Mars threatens us with the force of war
and will cause blood to be spilt seventy times.
The clergy will be both exalted and reviled moreover,
by those who wish to learn nothing of them.

Many of these non-rhyming poems mentioned places in France, and they talked about disasters, like plagues and earthquakes. There were invasions, murders, battles, droughts, floods, and war. But, I had difficulty to connect them with specific events in the real world.

Another one said,

Garden of the world near the new city,
In the path of the hollow mountains:
It will be seized and plunged into the Tub,
Forced to drink waters poisoned by sulfur.

What would poisoned sulfur water taste like? Maybe like dark purple and black, or like eating piles of rotten oranges like we sometimes had in our orange grove?

Indeed, these four-line poems gave me interesting things to think about, but after finishing the book, I couldn't see how Nostradamus had predicted any event before it happened. Everything was in mystical terms that could apply to almost anything.

When finished reading the book, my mind filled with a myriad of contrasting colors, brick reds, and turquoise greens. Was it true what Maria said? There was little to connect me with Nostradamus. But, Maria was not definite and only suggested the connection.

When I thought about my own predictions, they were not about vague wars and droughts. Instead, my predictions were specific. They went somewhere and had an end, such as a horse crossing a line in front of the others.

I put the book back in my suitcase, now knowing that Nostradamus and I were not the same.

At least that one was solved. Maria's assumptions were incorrect. Having discovered that, I drifted back into a murky void while questioning my next move.

* * *

For seven days we crossed the Mediterranean, going from place to place. I mostly stayed on the deck at the front of the boat but did walk around occasionally to stretch my legs.

Staying at the front also meant that the seaman with the tight shifty eyes did not come near me, for he would be seen by anyone in the steering cabin.

But, the last evening before arriving in Genoa, I walked to the back of the boat and sat on the coil of ropes and watched the sunset. Then, the night darkened.

The Christobol moved north along the coast of Italy, and we passed villages. Groups of small fishing boats often floated stationary in the sea with bright lights to attract the fish.

Being tired, I fell asleep, and it must have been some hours later when I felt something moving in one of my front pants pockets.

My eyes opened, and someone crouched next to me. I grabbed the wrist of the hand in my pocket and yanked it, and it came out holding some of my dollars.

The night was black, but some light came from the small deck lights on the Christobol. It took a moment to see that the hand belonged to the seaman with the tight eyes.

He said, "Give me the money, or I throw you over."

A bold purple filled the air, and I stood up and said, "Iwo Jima."

"What?"

We faced each other. "Iwo Jima," I cried out. "You are a buzzard."

He stopped for a moment, eyes wide, then stated, "You speak crazy. Give me the money."

He lunged for me, but the years of running in the orange grove had made me quick. He held my dollars in one hand and reached for me with the other. Each time he sprang toward me, I dodged away.

We moved along the rail until arriving at the end of the boat, and I sensed he was becoming angry, for his grunting sounds became more raspy and prologed each time he attacked me.

At the very back of the deck I got cornered, and even in the darkness of the night, I saw the constricted gleam of his smile. He reached for me and I lost my balance on the slippery deck and slipped onto my back. He paused for a second and grinned again, something like Al's grin, but with satisfaction, and then he dove toward me. I pushed up with my legs, my feet kicking against his waist, and like two acrobats in a circus, my legs moved him forward, and in one smooth movement his momentum took him over the rusty rail.

He tried to grab the rail with his free hand, but it slithered, and he flew down toward the dark water. Releasing the dollars, they fluttered like birds in the backdraft of the Christobol.

The splash of his body blended with the white churn behind the Christobol and his head went under, and then he popped up and gasped for air. He shook his fist at me and then began swimming a breast-stroke. He needed training for the timing of the kick of his legs, and the thrust of his arms was not in sink, but at least he moved forward.

Not far away there were at least fifteen small fishing boats clustered near each other, and I saw him heading toward them, his body seen in the shimmer in their bright reflecting lights. I suspected he would reach those boats, but wondered more about where he learned to swim. Was it in a swimming pool where he touched the tiles and spit in the gutter? He definitely needed more lessons.

If he wasn't rescued by the boats, it was inevitable he would be swallowed by the depths of the dark sea. Then, what would happen? Fish food.

CHAPTER 27

I slept that night on the coiled rope, for it was more comfortable than the hammock in the tight room. The air was fresher. I also figured that if any more seamen tried to take my money, they'd end up like the one with the tight eyes.

In the morning, I awoke to the pale light coming from the east. My first thought was for the seaman with the tight eyes and what happened to him, but that didn't last for long. Instead, my primary consideration was where I should go when we arrived in Genoa. Should it be to Marseille and the village of Nostradamus, or somewhere else?

While considering the options, when thinking of Marseille, a dark cloud appeared, like that emanating from the Guardia Civil. Then I saw a lawn-green stream going in another direction.

I went up to the steering cabin to find Captain Pujols.

As I walked in he smiled and asked, "How you do?"

"I slept well," I said and then pointed at the map on the wall and asked, "Do you have a map of the entire sea?"

He laughed. "You want the world?"

"No, just this sea here."

"You point at it, on the wall."

"But, where is Greece?" I asked.

"Greece?"

"It isn't there on the map."

He shook his head and went to a large drawer under the table, and there was a stack of maps. He took one out and laid it on the table."

I looked intently at it but didn't see Greece.

He pointed his finger to Genoa and said, "We are going there, maybe dock in one hour." He drew his finger across the map toward the east, crossing Italy, and then sliding over a blue sea until it stopped at a piece of land. Then he circled his finger around what seemed to be hundreds of islands. "That's Greece.

Why you want to know?"

"Because I need to find out about John who lived on an island called Patmos. Can you help me?"

* * *

In Genoa, Captain Pujols took me to a travel agency near the port and introduced me to an older woman whose name was Annetta Allegra. They spoke in Italian, and even though I didn't understand them, the sound of their words gave off a musical, light cyan blue.

Finally, they stopped talking, and Annetta looked at me and said, "So, you want to go to Athens?"

"No. I want to go to Patmos. I think it is an island."

Captain Pujols raised his hands, palms pointed upwards and looked at the woman. She raised her eyebrows. Then he turned to me and asked, "Why there? There is nothing on Patmos."

"I want to see where someone lived."

"Why?" He asked.

"Because my friend Maria said I am like this person."

"That is funny," Captain Pujols said.

Annetta raised her right hand in the air, fingers pinched. "Sure. I can get you anywhere. I can even hide you anywhere in the world if you want."

She worked out an itinerary to go by train from Genoa to Milan, and then a flight to Athens.

Then she opened a book with a map of Greece and said, "We can find small flights to the island of Leros, and from there you can take a boat to Patmos."

Captain Pujols said, "Leros has good port. Long history. Romans, Crusaders, Turks, and British have all been there. Narrow opening but deep water. Very good. It is not far from Patmos. In Patmos, there is nothing."

The thought of all this travel created a confusing mix of

colors, and they only got more turbulent when I considered all the flights. I asked, "Is it possible to take a boat from Athens?" A green stream pushed the mix of colors into the background.

She answered, "Yes, many boats leave Athens for Greek islands. I can arrange for you to take a tourist boat."

Captain Pujols laughed. "Or cargo boat like mine."

A tourist boat meant encountering many passengers, and the conflicting mix of colors returned, overpowering the lawn-green stream. The choice was clear. "I want a cargo boat," I said.

Annetta's eyes opened wide. "A tourist boat would be much better with good food and a good bed."

"No," I stated, seeing the green stream taking me somewhere. Having made the cargo boat decision, the stream now changed to something that was clear like glass or crystal.

Captain Pujols smiled and asked Annetta, "May I have paper and pencil?"

She gave him a blank piece of paper and a pencil, and he wrote something and handed it to me. "That is contact for Stelos Antonopoulos. He is boss at Piraeus Maritime, which makes schedules for cargo boats. Piraeus is port city for Athens, and many cargo boats in Greece take tourists, only five or ten at a time. Mostly people sleep on deck with blankets and sacs."

"Sleeping bags?" I asked.

"Yes, if that is what you call them."

The translucent, crystal green stream had widened, and it was almost a river.

Captain Pujols had to leave, and I thanked him like Maria had taught me. Annetta instructed me to sit in a chair while she made several phone calls, and then she went to a drawer where she took out airline tickets, and she wrote my name and the flight numbers on them.

She arranged for her nephew go with me by train to Milan and then to the airport. I would be lost without having assistance, and it made me think about again finding someone like Maria. It was helpful to have a helper.

I paid Annetta Alegra for the train and flight tickets using my American Express Travelers Cheques, and I realized not many remained.

Finally, she said, "How old are you?"

"Thirteen, but almost fourteen."

"Oh, mamma mia. Questo è pazzesco." She raised her fingers pointing upwards, and it seemed a gesture I should practice.

"What does that mean?" I asked.

"It means, Mamma mia this is crazy."

That seemed a good phrase to remember, *Questo è pazzesco.* "Can you teach me to use my fingers like you do?"

"What is this?" She asked.

CHAPTER 28

Three days later I was on a cargo boat in the Aegean Sea. Its name was Ambrosia, which Stelos Antonopoulos said meant immortal. He said that in Greek mythology, ambrosia is the name of a food or drink of the gods that gives them immortality. I wished so, for the Ambrosia looked like anything but that.

Captain Pujol's boat, the Cristobol, was a luxury liner in comparison to the Ambrosia. When my grandfather spoke about a car as a rust-bucket, that accurately described this boat, for there was hardly any paint anywhere. When you held the rails, it felt like rough gravel. The smokestack was on the back of the boat, and clouds of dark-gray smoke billowed up leaving a long trail into the distance behind us.

There were four other passengers on board along with five or six crew members. I didn't know the exact number of crew members for after the first stop at an island called Egina, three of the crew got off, and two new ones got on. Then at the next island, the same thing happened again. It looked like the Greek crewmen on the boat were merely using it to get from one place to another.

The first thing I had done when getting on the Ambrosia was to look where they kept the lifejackets. After an hour of searching, I found a rusted metal box toward the back of the boat containing lifejackets. Most were moldy and rotten. There were two lifeboats on the Ambrosia, and it was questionable if they could stay afloat.

Then I looked for a place to settle in.

When I got up to the main deck, there were four travelers there who looked to be in their late teens and early twenties, three guys and a girl. The girl seemed younger than the guys, but I'm not good at guessing ages. They already rolled out their sleeping bags and had taken places sheltered from the wind.

When they saw me, one of them said, "It looks like nursery school is on holiday." He had a British accent which I recognized from my time in London.

All the guys laughed.

"What's your name, kid?" He asked.

"Arlo. What is yours?" I smiled as Maria had taught me and then I gave him the Al smile.

He turned to the girl and asked, "What is this, a kiddy freak show?"

She looked at me for several seconds and then at the guy and said, "Hugh, lay off him." Then she whispered something in his ear.

Hugh chuckled and said, "Jill, yeah. He doesn't look right." He turned to me, and his eyes had a challenging kind of look, like the teens in the swimming pool back home, and he asked, "What are you doing on this boat? Are you lost?"

"I'm not lost," I said.

One of the other guys spoke up and asked. "How old are you?"

He had a different kind of accent, and I guessed he was from Germany or someplace around there.

"I'm thirteen, almost fourteen."

"And someone lets you travel by yourself?" He asked.

"My uncle Louie is responsible for me."

"And where is he," the girl asked.

"In New York, in an insane asylum."

They all stayed quiet for a good bit and then they looked at each other and started laughing. I didn't know why because I had truthfully answered their questions. The reactions and body language of people were often difficult to interpret.

"Well, this is going to be a fun trip. Find a place," Hugh stated."

All the protected places were taken by the other travelers, so I put my suitcase against a wall that was in the sun and directly hit by the wind. In Piraeus, I had purchased a blanket, as none of the shops sold sleeping bags. That was placed next to the suitcase. I also had a paper bag with a glass bottle with water and some crackers.

Stelos Antonopoulos had informed me that the cargo boat didn't serve food, but it did have a head, which he explained was the nautical term for a bathroom. There were only a toilet and a small sink in there, but nowhere to take a shower.

If it rained or if it got too cold at night, then we could shelter in a long corridor inside the boat, but most of the time we had to stay on the front part of the upper deck.

Stelos also said that the boat made frequent stops, sometimes visiting two or more islands per day. The stops gave enough time to buy food, and on some stops, there was enough time to go to a restaurant. He said the captain would always tell us how long the boat would dock.

After I made myself at home on the deck, I imagined that I had done a good thing. I still didn't know if it was the right thing because I wasn't sure what was right and wrong for this kind of decision.

All I saw was a green crystal river going before me, so my journey seemed like a correct choice, like picking the right horse. Yet, way off in the distance, I saw the faint sliver of something not entirely describable, which some might call menacing, like a storm shadow.

As I looked off into the horizon and saw my crystal river shimmering above the deep blue Adriatic Sea, I wondered what this all meant. Ever since falling out of my grandfather's oak tree I had these perceptions. They were useful in predicting outcomes of horse racing and stock market movements, but now I sensed they were relevant to other things.

In Chicago at Mario's bucket shop I saw dark clouds and ran away from the detective and police officers, quickly following the river out of the building. Was that a prophecy or just some kind of reaction?

Why did I perceive the dark baseball mitt over Maria's head, like I knew something was going to happen? In the travel agency in Genoa, why had I seen the lawn-green river direct me toward a cargo boat in Athens rather than a tourist ship? Was that only because of my aversion to crowds of people?

In the ads in the Los Angeles newspaper, Napoleon Hill said you could think and grow rich. I knew I could do that. It was probably all I was good at, to think and guess stock market movements. But, was I able to predict other things?

In looking across the Adriatic Sea, I wondered if that faint menacing sliver on the horizon was an indication of something important about to happen?

CHAPTER 29

After leaving Athens, the boat wandered from island to island. The two Germans got off in Mykonos, a place where there were windmills and many tourists.

I rotated through the two business suits that Maria had chosen for me, and they were getting wrinkled. In Mykonos, some of the tourist shops sold clothing, mainly white cotton pants and white shirts like those worn by some of the Greeks. I bought a pair of pants and a shirt, which were more comfortable than the business suits. The jackets of my business suits worked just fine when it got windy or a little bit cool.

I also purchased a hat like those worn by sailors on Greek ships. Hugh laughed when he saw me in my new clothing.

Greeks and other nationalities used the Ambrosia to go from one place to another, like a taxi going to the next island. I learned things from them. For instance, the younger Americans and British were known as *backpackers,* and they called this *island hopping.*

The two British, Hugh and Jill stayed on the boat. They were traveling together but were not married. When I asked them if they were boyfriend and girlfriend Hugh laughed and said, "That's such outdated terminology. We are travelers like Jack Kerouac, free spirits, and that's it."

As he said that, I noticed that Jill's cheeks become a color I couldn't directly identify, somewhere between pinkish red and candy apple red. It was one manifestation of being embarrassed or ashamed. Maria had taught me to recognize that when looking at facial expressions.

Jill was eighteen years old and had just finished the English equivalent of high school, which was called A Levels or O Levels. She was taking a year off before starting university and wanted to go into medicine, perhaps nursing.

Hugh and Jill met on a boat crossing the English Channel and had been traveling together since then, for about three weeks. Hugh was older than Jill, and it seemed he had control of her, for he told her where they would go, what they would do, and he often contradicted what she said.

Jill's face often turned into smiles when she saw me, and for some unknown reason, it seemed she wanted to protect me. She reminded me of Maria, but not in every way. Maria was much older, thin, and with wrinkled skin. A presence extruded from Maria like colorful music notes gently relaxing the world around her.

Jill was different. She carried kindness like Maria, but one sensed that she hadn't fully considered the consequences of her choices, nor the implications of her immediate flow of history. Physically she had blond hair and blue eyes, like other people in the UK. Her skin was brown from the sun, although once when she bent over, and her shirt moved up, I saw that the skin on her lower back was pearly cream.

There was something about Jill that was fresh and vibrant, yet I saw a thin gray weight on her shoulders, and more weights floated above her like they were ready to drop on her one at a time.

When the two Germans left the Ambrosia at Mykonos, I moved my blanket and suitcase to their place on the deck. It was secluded and out of the wind.

Shortly after the boat departed from Mykonos, I heard Hugh say, "Well, we got rid of the two Krauts."

"I looked across the eight or ten feet space that separated us and asked, "What's a Kraut."

He laughed, in a way that was more of an attack than expressing happiness. "You don't know anything."

Jill said, "Quit coming down on the kid."

"Shut up," he said. "You're just like all the other birds. Empty-headed."

"Why are birds empty-headed?" I asked.

He laughed again, only this time harder and even more attacking. "That just shows you don't know anything. Birds are girls."

Then I remembered that Louie also called them birds, but Hugh and Louie were wrong. Things are what they are. A car is not a horse. A girl is not a bird. A boy is not a girl, so I said, "No they're not. Birds have feathers, and they fly. Girls can't fly."

He shook his head. "Kid, you need to learn about the world. Is this your first trip?"

"No. I've been across America two times and to London and Paris and Spain."

"That's a good start," he said. "I've been all over Europe and Africa. Been doing it for five years."

"How do you live?"

"What do you mean?"

"How do you pay for it?"

"British welfare. It funds me, always has and always will. Why work when the government pays for you."

When he said that, his words streamed out like small purple fires and they floated up and spread into his hair.

"I don't know anything about that," I said.

He grinned. "A kid in your condition could easily get welfare, the strange way you look at things and that walk. You could milk a fortune from that."

Jill commanded, "Hugh. I keep telling you to quit pushing Arlo. He can't help it what he is."

"Maria tried to help me act normal," I stated.

"Who is Maria," Jill asked.

"She's dead. She had a wounded heart and died in a church in Sudanell in Spain, but the Guardia Civil think I did it and they are looking for me."

Hugh said, "How about that. We are traveling with a fugitive.

Did you kill her?"

The purple fires were still in Hugh's hair, like colorful maggots competing for space. "No, she fell forward and died."

Hugh turned to Jill and said, "Keep an eye on him for no telling what he might do."

Hugh's comment was interesting, and part of it was correct. How do you know what anyone will do, but why do you need to keep an eye on them? More than that, when he spoke, I saw him as a little buzzard milking British Welfare. It seemed that buzzards were everywhere, taking what belongs to others.

After that we all got quiet, and I read a book. Travelers exchanged books, as reading material was difficult to come by. Having read The Prophecies several times, I still wasn't getting anything out of it with its vague sayings that could be twisted to apply to just about anything.

So, I had traded The Prophecies for a copy of Cannery Row by John Steinbeck and then traded that for a copy of The Catcher in the Rye by J.D. Salinger. Each book produced different colors. Cannery Row extruded a dark brown and turquoise blue, like earth and sea existing beside each other. The best way to describe The Catcher in the Rye was like a slow-moving pinball randomly moving through a forest with no paths.

Maria's Holy Bible was still in my suitcase. I wanted to hold off reading it until I got to Patmos where John lived. Every time I opened my suitcase, the book gave off a translucent light blue cloud.

The colors and images I see are impossible to accurately describe to others, but they are real to me.

CHAPTER 30

Over the following days, we went from Mykonos to Paros and then to Heraklion in Crete. From the map in the captain's steering cabin, Crete was in the south of Greece.

One time Hugh laughed at me when I said "captain's steering cabin," and I learned from him that the official name for the steering cabin is called the wheelhouse.

Patmos was on the North-East side of Greece quite close to Turkey, and we gradually zigzagged through the islands in that direction.

Sometimes when we stopped, I put on my swim trunks and went for a swim, as a way of taking a bath. I found that being in the sea gave tranquility and it softened colors.

Once I tried to wash my pants and shirt in the sea for they had become stained, but when they dried, they became stiff like cardboard.

Several times I asked the captain if the Ambrosia was stopping in Patmos and he always raised his eyebrows, looked to the sky, took a deep breath and answered, "Of course."

From Heraklion, we went east to the remote island of Karpathos, and the crew spent a day and a half doing repairs on the engine of the boat. That gave me time to walk on land.

I had meals in small restaurants where they allowed you to go into the kitchen and point to what you want, as the menu was in Greek and could not be understood. On Karpathos, people dressed differently than on the other islands and Jill explained to me that this was "traditional dress." In other words, it was clothing from the old days.

A new captain came onto the Ambrosia at Karpathos. He was a dark-skinned man who looked like he had spent many years in the sun. His beard was a mix of black and gray. His shirt was open in the front, and you could see his hairy chest and a large belly.

The first time I went to the wheelhouse to talk with him, he smelled of alcohol, as did some of the new crew. They drank something called Ouzo, always having a glass of it before and after every meal. Hugh often joined them, although he drank more than the others. Ouzo was not expensive, and Hugh had purchased four bottles of it in a shop in Karpathos.

We turned north toward the direction of Patmos but there were a lot of islands, and the Ambrosia stopped at many of them. I had now been on the Ambrosia for over two weeks and was tired of sleeping on a hard deck. Being anxious to get to Patmos I went to the wheelhouse to ask how long it would take to get there.

"Patmos?" The Captain asked. "We are not going to Patmos. There is nothing there."

That was of interest, as I spotted a contradiction. So, I asked, "How can people say one thing and then do another?"

"You speak riddles. I am not going to Patmos."

"But Stelos Antonopoulos said the Ambrosia was going to Patmos, and so did the previous captain."

"Stelos doesn't know everything."

I found that to be an accurate statement. No one knows everything. "But, I need to go to Patmos."

"Why? There is nothing there."

"Because I want to learn about John. I may be like him."

"I don't know this John. Anyway, in Greek it is *Ioannes*."

"He lived there, in Patmos," I stated.

"Where is he now?"

"Dead."

"Then it is foolish to go to a place where the person you wish to visit is dead and anyway there is nothing on Patmos."

How could I tell this man that what he said made logical sense, except a green river was leading me there? "How can I get there?" I asked.

He looked at the map on the table and said, "Late tonight we arrive at Leros. Boats go from there to Patmos, mainly tourist boats. It might take several days, but you can find a boat on Leros."

As he said it, there was a blackish cloud that arose from him, not exactly a baseball mitt but more like a hand holding a hammer.

* * *

For over an hour I stood at the bow of the ship looking at the horizon, at the narrow line that separated sea and sky, their colors almost the same with only a slight distinction. The hand on the hammer gave me something to think about, and I deduced that it was like the dark mitt. Something extreme was about to happen.

Then when I looked at the horizon again, I noticed the gray silver line that I had seen before, only this time it was slightly bigger and moving. Once in the orange grove, my grandfather killed a rattlesnake, cutting its head off with a shovel. The headless snake twisted and writhed, and there was something like that in the gray silver line. I wasn't sure what to make of it.

I went back to my blanket and suitcase and suddenly had an impression that something was going to happen to the boat. It was a puzzling sensation.

Jill came to her sleeping bag, and her eyes were red and watery.

"Are you okay?" I asked. Maria had taught me that this is one of the phrases you should use when someone had red eyes and tears.

"No."

"Oh," I said, not sure what you are supposed to say after that.

She looked at me and laughed. "Arlo, you are sweet."

"You mean I taste like sugar or candy?"

She laughed, more like a small whimper that was almost a cough. "It's Hugh. He is drinking and saying terrible things."

I knew about drinking because of Louie. "Is he drunk?"

"It seems so. He is with some of the crew, and they are playing cards and drinking Ouzo. Someone said it's a drink that makes you crazy."

Uncle Louie had told me there were two kinds of drunks, happy drunks and mean drunks. I suspected that Hugh was the mean kind. "Is he saying angry things?"

She stayed silent for a moment, looking at the dark oil stained deck in front of us. "Cruel and threatening."

I said, "My experience is to stay out of the way until they sleep it off. If you try and reason with them, it doesn't go anywhere."

She looked me in the eyes, and I tried to stay focused on her, as Maria instructed. My habit was to look away, and I struggled to maintain contact. Then I wondered if I was staring.

She asked, "Did you have experience with this?"

"Some."

"A family member?"

"My uncle. He is now in upstate New York at the Hope Clinic trying to get some help."

"I'm sorry to hear that."

To be sorry was not one of my emotions and I tried to understand what she meant by it. Then I perceived that the silver line on the horizon was telling me something specific and I said, "The boat is going to sink."

"What? You mean this boat?"

"Yes. The Ambrosia."

"Arlo, have you done something? Did you mess with the engine?"

"No. Somehow I know the boat is going to sink."

"How can you tell that?"

"Because I see the future, not all of it, but some of it."

"I don't believe you." She stated.

"Okay," I responded.

"That's it? You don't react or get angry or feel hurt because I said I don't believe you?"

"No. I don't feel emotions, at least like other people. When cruel things are said to me, it doesn't cause me to get angry or sad or anything like that."

"You mean that all the nasty things Hugh has said to you have not made you irritated or want to get even with him."

"Not really. I see him more for what he is, like a buzzard?"

"A buzzard?"

"Yes, someone who takes from others, like taking from the British Welfare and how he is taking your soul."

She glanced away, and her neck and cheeks became red. "I hadn't thought about that."

The oncoming event came back to me, and I said, "But you know, the boat is going to sink."

"This rusty old thing is bound to sink one day."

"It will."

Her eyes were not as red, and I asked, "Are you better?"

"Yes, Arlo. Talking with you helped me recover a bit, and it gave me something to think about."

"About the boat?"

"No. About Hugh."

I wasn't sure what she meant by that, for why should anyone give a second of thought about Hugh? The Ambrosia was of far more interest.

CHAPTER 31

During the following hours, I stayed at my sleeping place on the deck. Having taken a loaf of bread and some dried ham out of my suitcase. I made a sandwich and began to eat it while thinking of where I was and where I had been.

In a way, this little place had become a home, a meek little corner on the deck of a rusted old cargo boat.

Soft colors and images had been with me during the past two weeks, unlike anything I'd ever experienced, except when doing my laps in our orange groves. If I understood the emotions behind the word, *like,* then maybe that's what I was experiencing.

It made me think of the people I had observed in Chicago, New York, and London, who scurried to get to their desks or trading stations each morning, and their frantic movements and shouting as the markets went up and down.

That didn't seem like a healthy way to live. Running an orange farm was preferable. Maybe even superior to that was being on a boat in the Adriatic Sea, feeling the warm wind against your face and watching the sunrises and sunsets.

Then, that thought made me realize that on my own I had made a judgment between better and worse. I always thought that you only learned the difference between good or bad when somebody told you. But now, I had realized something on my own.

Then I had another realization, like a magnificent display of fireworks. I may be the only person in the world who sees colors and images, not only in the words that come from the mouths of people but in just about everything I experienced. And most interesting is that those colors and images push out into future events.

That thought made me want to learn more about this John who lived on Patmos. Purposely I had not opened Maria's Holy

Bible to learn about John's Revelation. Maria said John's book was the last book in the Bible. That confused me, for the Bible was a book yet was made up of many books. That didn't make sense, for a book is a book and is not made up of many books.

I had not opened the Bible because I had seen a light blue glow coming from it like it was unique. The logic was, to fully appreciate the book, it seemed the book should be read at the place where it was written. But that was a limited logic, for if you applied that to every book, then you would spend a lifetime going from place to place reading books. For instance, where did John Steinbeck write Cannery Row? And, where did J.D. Salinger write The Catcher in the Rye?

In any case, I now wanted to get to Patmos as quickly as possible, and I wondered how I might find a boat at Leros that could take me there.

The day ended, and in the west, the sunset showed shades of carnation pink, fluorescent orange, and crimson red. I followed the evolution of the colors, absorbing detailed tones. Then the night became black, and the sky filled with a blanket of stars that descended to the horizon.

Then on the horizon in front of the boat, I saw the silver line, but it was no longer a line, for it rose upwards like reddish silver flames, long fingers that reached across the sea and grabbed the boat and took it down below the water.

To our right, was the outline of an island with the lights of some houses. I assumed that was Leros and remembered the few words that Captain Pujols on the Cristobol had said about it, that it had a deep-water harbor with a narrow opening.

The long silver fingers continued to reach toward the boat to pull it down, and at that moment I was confident that the Ambrosia was going to sink.

I considered the complications of this. The first alternative I thought of was that everyone on the boat would sink with it and drown and die. When I thought of my grandfather and Maria, I remembered the light translucent gray clouds that had surrounded them. We might all receive this.

Yet, I knew that I could swim and the shoreline of Leros was not that far away. I could make it. Could the others swim?

Only, I probably couldn't swim to the island while pulling a water-soaked suitcase and Maria's Holy Bible would become wet and unreadable. Did that matter?

Yes, it did, for could I find another Bible in English anywhere on Leros or on Patmos? Probably not.

I needed that Bible, for I needed to find out about John. Then I wondered if John had a last name, what some called a family name, All the people I had ever met had a last name, but what about John? I'd find out, but for now, he would be known as John Patmos for lack of something better.

The boat was getting closer to the shoreline, and there was a small light flashing near some rocks.

Across from me, Jill slept on top of her sleeping bag, because the night was warm.

I got up and made my way to the back of the boat, and in the reflected light, I found the box with the lifejackets. After rummaging through it, I found two that were still intact and not too rotten.

I put one on and went back to Jill and shook her shoulder with my hand.

Her eyes opened, and she mumbled, "What is it, Arlo?"

"The boat is going to sink?"

"What?" She asked.

"The boat is going to sink. Put this on."

She slowly sat up. "Arlo, what are you talking about?"

"Do you remember how I told you that I can see things before they happen?"

"I remember, but I don't believe you."

"You must trust me, now. Put this on, take your things and go to the lifeboat." I handed her the second lifejacket.

She stood up, reached down and took her sleeping back and backpack. Then she took a few steps toward the direction of the lifeboat, stood still and turned around. "Arlo, are you crazy." She asked.

"Not like Uncle Louie," I said.

She said, "Oh my. What am I doing?" Then, she continued along the walkway.

I picked up my suitcase and blanket and followed along behind her, and when we got to the lifeboat, I put our things inside. "Wait here," I said.

I made my way back along the walkway, went up the stairs that led to the wheelhouse, opened the door and went inside.

Around the chart-table, sat all the members of the crew including the captain. Hugh was passing a bottle of Ouzo to one of the crew members. It was half full. Three empty Ouzo bottles were on the floor next to Hugh.

They were all laughing, words slurring from their mouths. A card game was in progress, and money was on the table. Immediately I thought of Uncle Louie and how he became when he drank too much. He lost a lot of money to the Mafia in New York, and I had to save him.

When they saw me enter the wheelhouse, Hugh said, "Wha-da ya want, idiot kid? Wanna play cards?" He took the half bottle of Ouzo, his hand swaying back and forth and he handed it in my direction. "Drink this."

I looked at the captain and said, "Something is going to happen."

"Wazzat?" Hugh said.

"The boat is going to crash on the rocks and sink."

"What is this?" The captain asked. He glanced quickly at me and then his eyes focused back on the cards in his hand.

"The boat is going to sink. All day I knew about it," I stated.

None of the crew members could speak English. One of them looked at the captain and said something in Greek.

The captain spoke back to him, and then they all looked at

me, and with the timing of a choir, they joined together in a loud roaring laugh.

The captain looked at me and said, "This boat never sink. Too old. Too much experience."

Hugh said, "Get lost. We got money on the table.

Calmly I said, "It is going to sink, soon."

I turned around and went back down the stairs to the lifeboat and saw Jill. She had released the boat from its fixation, and it was swung away from the cargo boat.

"They are drunk, and they don't believe me," I said.

"Me neither, I don't believe you. I must be senseless to do this," she exclaimed.

"No, get in. In a few minutes, the boat will hit rocks near the entrance of the harbor." The reddish silver fingers were most intense, about two hundred yards ahead on the right side of the boat.

Jill asked, "Do you think we can drop the lifeboat while the cargo boat is still moving?"

"Maybe," I said. "The Ambrosia isn't moving very fast."

We got into the lifeboat and Jill released two ropes, and we each took one and then lowered the lifeboat into the water. The lifeboat scooted alongside the Ambrosia until we released the ropes, and then the lifeboat fixation lines dangled down in front of us, and we floated free. Quickly, we were left behind.

The cargo boat distanced itself from us and headed into darkness, as its diesel engine rumbled. Our lifeboat tilted back and forth in the wake of the more massive vessel.

The Ambrosia went forward for about two hundred yards, and then there was a deep groaning sound as the boat came to an agonizing stop, rusty metal crunching against rocks. Then it stayed stationary while trying to keep its balance. I knew that wobbly sensation.

The Ambrosia tilted, and loud rattling sounds came from lose cargo moving within the hull. And then the Ambrosia slanted further, and it half sunk against the rocks of Leros.

The only sounds were metal clanking against metal, like the ringing of a death bell, but that stopped, and there was only the sound of the sea lapping against the side of our lifeboat. The Ambrosia's lights went out and the black canopy of night engulfed us.

CHAPTER 32

Gradually my eyes adapted to the darkness and I watched Jill reach along the inside of the lifeboat. She took out two sets of oars, placed them in holders along the sides of the lifeboat, and then she sat on a long wooden seat and instructed me to sit on the seat behind her.

I held onto one set of oars, and she took the other.

"Do you know how to row?" She asked.

"No, but I know how to swim."

"That's good because this lifeboat might sink."

I noticed some water down by my feet.

She demonstrated how to row, lifting the oars out of the water, bending forward, dropping the oars and then pulling backward. We practiced a few strokes until I learned it.

"That's good," she said. "Now, let's head for the harbor."

It was slow going, but after a while, we got into a cadence, and we went around the west side of the Ambrosia. For something that had been so alive, the boat now seemed dead, only I didn't see the same gray glow from it that emanated from my grandfather and Maria.

"Are they alive?" Jill asked.

"Who?" I asked. I had been thinking of my grandfather and

Maria, and of course, they were not alive.

"Hugh and the captain and crew. What happened to them?"

"I don't foresee everything," I replied.

"No, Arlo, what is your guess?"

"I'm not sure I ever guess."

"Please try."

I looked at the Ambrosia, half sloping in the water, the upper decks now seen from a new angle. The wheelhouse was out of the water. "They might still be in there. They were drunk as skunks."

"Arlo, I'd like to laugh, but I'm in shock. Where did you learn that about drunk as skunks?"

"From my grandfather when he met Louie in the backyard after Louie had been screaming about Iwo Jima and Japs."

"Japs is not the right thing to say."

"That's what Louie called them."

"I know, but we don't speak like that anymore."

We quit discussing and continued to row, and came around to the entrance of the harbor. Four small fishing boats were headed our way. They had lights hanging on metal poles on the sides, like Coleman lanterns that you put paraffin in and then pumped up.

Someone yelled out something in Greek.

Jill shouted back, "Do you speak English?

One of the men yelled, "Yes. A little."

"The Ambrosia hit the rocks and sunk."

"The Ambrosia?" He exclaimed.

"Yes."

The man translated to the others, and then they all laughed.

"Why do they laugh," Jill yelled out.

The man shouted back. "That boat should never be on the sea. All people on the Greek islands knew this day would come. Where is captain and crew?"

"We don't know. Maybe still on the boat," she said with a loud voice.

Three of the fishing boats headed around the entrance of the harbor in the direction of the Ambrosia and one stayed behind with us. They fixed a line from their boat to our boat, and then they pulled us to the docks.

It was one o'clock in the morning, and one of the fishermen led us to a small hotel and knocked on the door. It took several minutes until a woman came. She only had one room with two beds, so we took it.

In the middle of the night, I heard Jill crying, for I suspected she was feeling emotions about what had happened. I didn't say anything, not wanting to interrupt her moment, so I went back to sleep.

In the morning, Jill's bed was empty, but her backpack and sleeping bag were still there. My suitcase and blanket were in the place I had put them.

I made my way down the hall to the bathroom, which was a small narrow room with a single toilet. In the room next to it was a sink and shower, so I undressed and took a shower and used soap to wash my hair. It was my first real shower since Barcelona.

Going back to our room, I dressed in my white pants and white shirt. Then I went downstairs, and there was a small room with tables, and some people were eating breakfast.

The lady that ran the place brought me coffee and bread and a large jar of tzatziki, which is a white cream with chives. The taste was like music notes from a classical song I once heard on the radio. I think it was from someone called Chopin, although I didn't learn his last name.

When finished with breakfast, I sat back and took a deep breath. And then Jill came in.

She walked quickly up to my table and said, "Arlo, we need to talk." She looked around at the people at other tables who were looking at her. The men looked at her up and down the same way that Louie looked at "pretty dames."

"Let's go to the room," she said.

When we got to our room, she spoke very fast. "Arlo, you need to get out of here. Last night the fishermen went to the Ambrosia, and they rescued the captain and Hugh, and the rest of the crew. As you said, they were drunk as skunks. They were banged up and hurt from the boat crash, and one of them has a broken arm. Anyway, a few minutes ago, Hugh and the captain woke up, and immediately Hugh said bad things. He claims you sunk the Ambrosia. The captain didn't say anything at first, but then he agreed with Hugh."

She was speaking so fast that I had a difficult time to interject. I said, "What they say is not correct. They were playing cards and drinking Ouzo and weren't watching where the boat was going. In fact, it was Hugh who encouraged them to drink. He is destructive. They drank practically four bottles of his Ouzo."

"You better get out of here," she said. "I found out that a luxury boat is leaving for Patmos in a few minutes. If you run, you can make it. Hopefully, they will take you."

I went to my suitcase and took out a wad of Greek Drachmas, maybe fifty dollars' worth or so, and handed the money to Jill. "For the hotel and for you."

She shook her head. "Arlo, I can't.

"Yes. Take it."

She took the money and said, "You need to go."

I picked up my suitcase and blanket and asked, "What will you do now?"

"Hugh has friends on the island. We were talking about staying here for a while because he had some business ideas here, a product to sell. That was lost last night on the Ambrosia. Now he is talking about continuing to travel, maybe to Turkey or North Africa."

I nodded, yet saw something dark when I looked at her, not a mitt, but something almost as sinister. It was like a vice from my grandfather's workshop, and she was in it. It slowly squeezed in such a way that she wouldn't notice it at first until it was too late.

We went down the stairs, for our room was on the upper floor and then she led me to a back door, and we went out and then scurried through some narrow streets, to the docks, until we came directly to a large white ship that was many times bigger than the Ambrosia.

We walked to the bottom of the gangplank, and no one was there. Jill said, "Go hide."

She grabbed my arm and pulled me to her and gave me a kiss on the cheek and said, "Arlo. Thank you. Take care of yourself."

The vice still hovered around her, and I said, "I see soft colors when I see you, but these will be squeezed and destroyed."

She had a quizzical look, one Maria had taught me to identify. Her head slightly tilted. One side of her mouth raised toward a cheek and one eyebrow somewhat elevated.

"What?" She asked.

"The color from your entire being is soft and brings life and peace, and a stream could take you to something special, but you must wake up to realize it. Otherwise, it will not be fulfilled."

She shook her head, short jerky movements, and then her eyes moistened. "Arlo, your riddles cut me to the core."

"I don't know riddles," I countered, "Only what will happen."

She took a deep breath and said, "Go quickly."

I sprinted up the gangplank like when I ran in the orange groves, and then made my way down a hallway while passing several people. They spoke French, which I recognized from my time in Paris.

Then I saw a door that said "storage" on it, so I opened it. It was a small room and had some mops, brooms, and buckets in one corner. Shelves were on one wall, stacked with bottles of bleach and soap.

I entered the room and shut the door and waited. It didn't take long until the ship's engines became louder and I sensed movement.

The darkness of the room pushed in on me, and I doubted if Jill was right. Was this ship headed for Patmos?

CHAPTER 33

The storage room was dark, so I opened the door a bit to let light in and then found a switch, and turned on a small light. I wasn't sure what to do. Everything happened so fast at Leros with Jill rushing me to this ship.

Something kept coming back to me. Jill had hugged me and gave me a kiss on the cheek and said thank you. Maria would have liked that, not only saying thank you but also showing that kind of emotion.

The hug and the kiss flooded me with a mix of colors, not only pinks but vibrant pastels that sent pulsations through my body. These would be kept in my memory to bring back again, if possible to find out what they meant.

Was this a new element in my discovery? It certainly had nothing to do with thinking and growing rich. Forecasting the sinking of the Ambrosia confirmed that my perception of colors and images was a way of forecasting events, beyond horse racing and stocks. But, what did those pastel colors mean? Did they have a direction?

When I visualized Jill, there was a complicated mix. Besides the dark, slow squeezing vice-grip, there was also an image I didn't recognize. It was like a pure white river.

Did I see something in her like I had seen with the Ambrosia? Did those colors forecast Jill's future, but why was there a such a striking difference between the two images of the dark vice-grip and the white river?

This required further reflection.

In the meantime, I needed to figure out if this ship was indeed headed to Patmos. I waited a while and then left my suitcase in the storage room and ventured out.

There were many people moving about. Most spoke French, but there were other languages.

I wandered around until I came to a large restaurant where people drank coffee and tea and ate those crescent-shaped pieces of bread that the French called croissants.

From a large rack of cups, I took one and served myself a coffee. I preferred it black rather than with cream and sugar. With black, there were more subtle flavors of berries and nuts, which evoked fascinating colors. Milk and sugar camouflaged those tastes.

Then I sat at an empty table and observed the people. It was noisy, particularly coming from the French, where the syllables of their words bouncing off the walls as machine gun bullets. The French were animated, and it seemed everyone talked at the same time, but no one got angry when others weren't listening.

I heard an older couple speaking English so got up went to them.

The man looked at me and asked, "Can I help you?" He had one of those British accents.

"Do you know where this boat is going?" I asked.

The man looked at the woman, who I assumed was his wife, for they both wore wedding rings. "I lost count of the places we have visited. What's next?"

From her bulky handbag, she took out a piece of paper, peered at it and said, "Patmos."

The man looked at me. "That's jolly good. Patmos is historical. Evidently, it was where they kept prisoners during the Roman times. It's a backwater place." He looked at the woman's piece of paper and said, "We arrive in two hours and will only be there four hours. After that, it's a straight run to Macedonia."

I thanked him and went back to my cup of coffee.

As I was drinking, I saw one of the crew members staring at me, and then he disappeared through a door. Somehow that triggered the flight colors, an ominous dark river tugging at me to get out of there, so I quickly finished my coffee and went out through a door on the opposite side of where the crewman had exited.

After walking down a hallway, another hallway branched off to the left. I peeked around it and saw the crewman. He was quickly walking with another man who wore a white shirt that had gold bars on the sleeves and shoulders. They were headed for the restaurant but on the opposite side from where I was.

I went back to the storage room, took my suitcase and sat down on it. To relax, I filled the room with the images of orange fields and our oak tree. But, that didn't last long. A branch of the oak tree grew and extended to the interior of my suitcase, so I opened it and underneath a shirt was the book Maria had given me.

From the book emerged a translucent door which slowly opened and beckoned me to go through it, yet I was reluctant to do so for it was leading to something much more significant than predicting horse races. But, it also sent vibrations like those transmitted from the oak tree, and therefore I questioned if the book was risky or even dangerous. I closed the suitcase, and when flipping the latch, it made a definitive click.

* * *

After what seemed several hours, the sound of the ship's engines changed, and the movement slowed. I knew that sensation, for that's how it felt when the Christobol and the Ambrosia approached a dock.

My goal now was to get to Patmos, yet the image of those two seamen on this ship gave me caution. I assumed they would have angry emotions if they found me.

There were a lot of people who would get off the ship to visit the island, so I decided to try and blend in with them.

I carefully opened the door of the storage room and peeked outside. People walked along the hallway, so I took my suitcase and joined in, leaving my blanket behind. It might look like I was stealing a blanket.

My senses were now on full alert, noticing every detail about the people, their heightened voices, the strides of their walk, and the stuffiness of the air in the hallway.

I finally came out into the open, feeling the warmness of the late morning with its dry, hot air that tempered peoples' senses and made them lazy. Maria had called this "siesta time."

That was all right for me if it helped to get off the ship.

Ahead, I saw the British couple from the restaurant, so I squeezed through several people and approached them.

They smiled when they saw me, and the man looked at my suitcase and asked, "Getting off?"

"Yes," I answered.

"For a Yank, this is a strange place to leave the boat," he remarked. "What are you doing here?"

"I want to learn about someone who lived on this island."

"That's interesting," the woman said. "May I ask, where are your parents?"

"My father is dead, and my mother lives in San Diego."

"Oh," she said. "Then who is looking out for you?"

"My uncle."

We made our way to the gangplank and then merged in with the people descending to the dock.

The man said, "These French are awful. They mob and push and don't know how to make a proper queue. I'll be glad when we are rid of them."

The woman put her hand on my shoulder, bent toward me and said in a soft voice, "The froggies are horrible."

"Are there frogs on this island? No one told me about that."

She laughed and said, "Not at all. I was speaking of these French people."

"Why would you call them frogs?" I asked.

"Ah," she turned to her husband. "Why is that?"

He shrugged his shoulders. "Because that's what we have always called them."

That seemed unusual, to call people something without knowing the reason.

They continued talking to me as we went down the gangplank and I was glad for that because it made it seem like I was part of their group.

We got to the dock, and when looking back at the ship, I saw the two crewmen who had rushed to the restaurant. They looked in my direction, and then one pointed at me. Words were exchanged, and they moved quickly, pushing through the crowd of people at the top of the gangplank.

I turned to the couple and said, "I need to go," and then, "thank you," as Maria had taught me.

There were two small restaurants with outside chairs and tables, so I went past the tables and into the restaurant and straight into the kitchen.

A cook was chopping carrots. He said something in Greek and I said, "I don't understand."

In English, he said, "Not time for eating. Come back in one hour.

I went back to the front door of the restaurant. Outside, the two crewmen ran past, and I saw a dark cloud extending in front of them and behind them, like a long electrical shadow going in two directions.

CHAPTER 34

The dark shadow was electric, and it brought back memories of my oak tree. As the two men scurried further down the street, the electrical intensity calmed. Their ship would be leaving in a few hours, so I needed a place to hide. But, even more important than that, was to learn about John. It is one thing to get to a place. It is another to figure out what to do once you are there.

At the back of the restaurant's kitchen was a door, and a lime green river led to it. I followed the river, and it guided me through narrow streets. The streets were paved with flat stones, and the grouting around the stones was painted white, producing a myriad of unique designs. I wanted to stop and contemplate each one, but the green river compelled me to move on.

It only took a few minutes to get to the edge of the village where there was a house with a sign on it, 'Cambio, Chambres, Zimmer, Rooms", so I knocked on the door and went inside.

A large round woman came down a hallway wiping her hands on her apron. Before I could say anything, she asked, "Chambre, Room?"

"Yes."

"You speak English?" She asked.

"Yes."

"Good. English is better." She smiled, one tooth missing on the top and one on the bottom.

"American?"

"Yes."

"It is fifty American cents for each night."

"How much for one week?" I asked.

"One week? Three dollars and fifty cents."

I learned from Louie to never accept the first offer, so I said, "How about two fifty?"

She laughed. "Two dollars and fifty cents is too little. We split in middle. Three Dollars is good."

I had thirty dollars cash on me so gave her three.

She led me to a room on the top floor of her house. While climbing the stairs, she asked, "How old are you?"

"Thirteen, almost fourteen."

"You are so young, and you travel with just you?"

"Yes."

"Too young to travel with just you," she declared. It was more like a judgment.

"Uncle Louie says I sometimes think like an old man," I said.

She stopped at the top of the stairs, breathing heavily. "Patmos is peaceful place. You be okay."

"Thank you."

"Why you come here?"

"To find out about someone named John. He wrote a book."

She laughed. "Here, John is everywhere, monastery, church, Cave of Apocalypse. Everything named after John. Every man born on island is named John. Tourists come to Patmos because of John. He is good for business."

I saw small fireworks. This John Patmos must have been a significant person.

She opened the door to a room and then gave me a key.

"Toilet and shower on next floor down. Don't use much water. Not much on Patmos. My name is Eleni if you need anything."

The room was sparse, emitting a pale blue atmosphere. It contained a metal frame bed, a beige tile floor, whitewashed walls and a small wooden cross hanging above the door. The man was not on the cross.

A small window opened to the south, and not far away, the dry hills were covered with olive trees. Groups of people from the tourist ship walked on a path to the south. When getting off the ship, I heard the British couple talking about visiting a historical cave on the island, which I assumed was the Cave of The Apocalypse. Eleni spoke of it, and it had something to do with John.

I shut the door to the room and decided not to go out until the tourist ship left. The British man said the vessel would leave in four hours, so there were still two hours to go.

It was a good time to start reading John's book. Was he really like me, as Maria had suggested? Indeed, I was not like Nostradamus. Maybe there was more to acquire from John?

I opened my suitcase, took out Maria's Holy Bible and sat back on the bed. Flipping to the back of the book I found the first page of John's Book of Revelation.

The first sentence of Chapter one said, *"The Revelation of Jesus Christ, which God gave unto him, to shew unto his servants things which must shortly come to pass; and he sent and signified it by his angel unto his servant John."*

My skin tingled, and a silver river leaped from the page and then shot out like a horse race going somewhere.

The third sentence, which logically had the number three in front of it, said, *"Blessed is he that readeth, and they that hear the words of this prophecy, and keep those things which are written therein: for the time is at hand."*

Vibrant pastel colors soared from the page, even more

sensational than those from Jane's kiss on my cheek. The writing was odd, with phrases and words such as *"to shew unto"* and *"blessed"* and *"readeth"* and *"therein."* John wrote in an odd way, but it was understandable.

It was like reading the Daily Racing Form. I couldn't put it down. When people spoke, I saw their words in streams and colors and images. With John's book, each word and sentence became images stacked upon images jumping from the page. Therefore, each description needed to be savored.

This was the first time I found writings that matched how I routinely perceived the world, yet it went far beyond my ordinary.

The first few chapters were about some churches and what would happen to them. In Chapter Four, the colors and images accelerated. It began with a door opening to heaven where someone magnificent sat on a throne, and he was *like jasper and a sardine stone and there was a rainbow round about the throne, in sight like unto an emerald.*

My simple room filled with pulsating landscapes beyond anything one would find in the Louvre Art Museum in Paris. They were like images from dreams, but not imaginations. They were alive and real.

Then, I understood that this splendid being was the same person who was nailed to Maria's cross. How he got from the cross to the throne I didn't know, but it was evident that he belonged on the throne for he was all powerful and glorious, and beyond all seen and unseen, yet so much a part of what is real.

As Maria said, he is holy perfection that lives and is among us.

My head spun, so I stopped there and closed the book for it was impossible to absorb all those images at one time. This was exceptional. It touched the here and now while extending past the ends of the universe. That is too much to experience at one moment in time.

Staying still on my bed, I took deep breaths and tried to calm myself, realizing it might take a lifetime to comprehend what was in John's book.

After a while, my heartbeat slowed, and I realized I was hungry, but that was secondary. The primary task was to learn more about John and his book.

When I had read those first four chapters, it made me seem small like a grain of sand lost in an infinite ocean. It was absurd for Maria to say that I was anything like this John from Patmos.

CHAPTER 35

I decided to stay at Eleni's guest house, for no rivers or images led to anywhere else. The modest room minimized complexity. There was enough of that in John's book. The window of the room provided light as well as a serene landscape of a path and olive trees. And, it was quiet. That's all I needed.

Over the following days, I developed a routine, which should have made things normal. But, they weren't. The weight of John's writing brought unsettling insights and I was mesmerized by its wonder.

Every morning I ate a simple breakfast in a courtyard of the guesthouse. Eleni served *koulouri,* a bread ring covered in sesame seeds, something like the bagels in New York City.

Then Eleni gave me a packed lunch of bread, sliced meat and cheese, which I put in a cloth bag along with Maria's Holy Bible. Then I'd wander off to see the island.

On the first day there, I visited the Cave of the Apocalypse, but something didn't seem right about it. The Orthodox priests said this was the place where John wrote his Book of Revelation. Tourists went there and crowded around postcards and religious objects, some carved in olive wood. That produced a gray fog, so I didn't spend time at the cave.

On the island, small trails led past vineyards and barren land. There were secluded beaches and every day I swam in the warm water.

But, much of my time was devoted to reading John's book. I read slow, a chapter a day, stopping at each sentence to not only understand the meanings in the words but to imagine and see beyond them. There was more information in this book than I had ever read in any newspaper. Often, I had to stop and catch my breath because of the panoramas of thrones and celestial beings.

On the sixth day of my stay on Patmos, I went to the top of a small hill that looks west over the sea.

Until then I had mostly predicted events because of historical momentum, like stock prices. But, that day I realized something different, and that produced a profoundly new understanding. It was that history is going somewhere. History was more than patterns and extrapolations of numbers. The flow of reality was not in circular random events. History has a purpose, and was in the process of being fulfilled.

In Chapter six of John's book, it talked about four horsemen on different horses, white, red, black and ashen colored. The four horses swept across the sea and across the world, like a thundering horserace where the final end was a great day of wrath and judgment followed by an eternal kingdom with the magnificent being on the throne.

It was like John was writing the Daily Racing Form but on an infinitely grander scale.

On the sixth day on Patmos, I realized that the end of history was not to cross a finish line at Santa Anita Racetrack or to buy or sell Penny J.C. on an individual day. These were small happenings, part of something magnificent in which all events in space and time came to a meeting point. This was followed by an eternal new beginning.

One can read words as words, or even thoughts, but it is something else when they touch the weighty parts of one's realization. To do this, one needs to pause and to ponder and visualize. It is not just to see, but to profoundly picture and internalize. That's how I reflected on John's writing, sentence by sentence, using imagination to envisage each personality, object and scene, sometimes spending hours watching one of John's events unfold. It was a powerful way to read this book, natural for me. I wondered if anyone else did the same.

The four horsemen brought war and death as a prelude to the day that all people will stand before this king on the throne and be judged according to his purity.

The image of this was spectacular, filling the land and sea around me with a multitude of streams and rivers flowing forward with some parting into the black river and disappearing over a chasm into eternal separation from light. Other streams moved toward a crystal river whose source was the throne. That flowed through a city with a tree infinitely more amazing than my oak tree.

That day on the hill in Patmos was a turning point. There, I understood how people are free to make choices, but they are not free to avoid the consequences of their decisions. Each decision, each action, and each event whether determined or undetermined fits into the current of history. History is not random drifting. It is going somewhere.

Each day I read a chapter, and on my twenty-second day on the island of Patmos, I read the final chapter. It said, there are those with clean robes that can enter the city and have access to the tree of life. Yet there are others who are kept outside They are *"dogs, and sorcerers, and whoremongers, and murderers, and idolaters, and whosoever loveth and maketh a lie."* Were some of these people the buzzards I had met?

I finished the last chapter and lightning flashed across the sky when I read, *"Let the one who is thirsty come, and let the one who wishes take the free gift of the water of life."*

Then it spoke of *The Scroll of Prophecy*, and suddenly I realized what was on that scroll.

Maria said I might be like John, but I'd never push it that far, for I could never write what he did. But, I profoundly connected with his words.

After twenty-two days on the island of Patmos, the green river reappeared, and it led me off the island and pointed to tasks to be accomplished, tasks going all the way back home to the oak tree.

It was time to leave. I saw a fog like yellow teeth gnarling on either side of the green river, and I knew I shouldn't wobble from what needed to be done.

CHAPTER 36

The next morning, I carried my suitcase down to the courtyard and had breakfast. When finished, Eleni came to my table, and she said, "I don't like to see you go. You are like a son."

"I must go," I said. "Thank you for everything."

I stood up, and she gave me motherly kisses on both cheeks, flamingo pinks and lavender blues, and she said, "You must promise to come back to Patmos to see me."

I said, "I will, every year until you are gone." That would be for nineteen years. The dark mitt was in the background. It was a promise to be kept for I didn't want to be like the liars kept out of the city, as John had described.

"Until I'm gone?" She asked.

"Yes, until you go to the eternal city."

She smiled, teeth missing. "Mister Arlo, you are different than the others that come here. I will wait each year for you."

I picked up my suitcase and headed for the port.

My promise to Eleni was a future goal to be achieved, like touching the side of the swimming pool, walking the path to the oak tree, or thinking to grow rich.

It was a ten-minute walk to the port, and along the way, I passed tourists going in the direction of the Cave of the Apocalypse.

In the distance, I saw someone walking fast, and I recognized her. It was Jill from the Ambrosia.

She saw me, and her eyes opened, and she smiled and ran up to me. At first, she hesitated and then came close to me and gave me a hug.

Mothers did this to their children at the park, and I always wondered what that would be like. Maria had hugged me, but Jill's was different. Jill's embrace gave an unusual sensation, like rose petals swirling around in the air.

"Oh Arlo, I'm so glad to find you," she stated.

"Are you here to see the cave?"

"No, I'm here to find you and warn you?"

"Warn of what?"

"It's Hugh. He's been saying things about you. The authorities came to question us about the sinking of the Ambrosia, and now there's an investigation. Hugh and members of the crew are blaming you, saying you did something to the boat. I knew you were on Patmos, so came to warn you."

"Are the authorities looking for me?"

"Yes. Hugh has convinced them you are guilty. He made up a story about you tampering with the ship's navigation system." She paused then asked, "Did you have anything to do with the sinking of the Ambrosia?"

"No. I only knew it was going to sink. The crew was drinking Ouzo, and the captain wasn't paying attention to where the boat was going."

"Well, I don't understand how you knew it would sink, but you are in danger."

"Why would you come here to tell me this?"

"To warn you." She hesitated. "And, Hugh and I are not getting on."

"I know," I stated. "He is going in a dark direction. I saw that during our days of travel on the boat."

She lowered her voice and looked right and left. "He had a significant amount of marijuana in his bag to sell to backpackers. He's angry it was lost when the boat went down."

"The loss of that won't stop him from being destructive," I stated.

She lowered her head. "I thought I loved him."

"Do you?"

"I don't know. No, I don't think so."

I observed the rivers of her history and understood she needed to make a choice. I said, "You are at a crossroads and need to make a decision. If you stay with him your life will be sad. Your other choice is to come with me."

"What?"

"Today I'm leaving Patmos, going to Athens and then to London. You can come with me."

"Today?"

"Right now," I stated.

"But, I have things back on Leros."

She carried a small bag, not the one she had on the Ambrosia. I asked, "What's more important, your things or your life? We can replace your stuff."

"Arlo, I don't have the money to pay for a boat to Athens and a flight to London."

"Don't worry about that," Seeing history beyond financial needs, I said, "I want you to go to New York with me, to help me. I will pay you."

She stood still, staring into my eyes with such an intensity that I had to look away. She asked, "Arlo, who are you?"

CHAPTER 37

We got to London, and I visited Mr. Parker at Lehman Brothers. My investments had done okay, maybe not as well as if I had been actively managing them, but at least the portfolio had grown a little.

When speaking with Mr. Parker, I now had more clarity on the direction of stock prices, like bends were removed from winding rivers.

Jill went to Bournemouth to see her parents and collect some clothing, and then we flew to New York and took a taxi to my apartment.

When we arrived at the apartment, I asked Jill to open the curtains as I didn't want to get too close to the window. The view made me dizzy, and it would take time to adapt to it.

When the curtains opened, she stood still and exclaimed, "That's magnificent."

I glanced out the window and saw Central Park and the multitude of lights spreading out in the distance. Then there was something new that I hadn't seen before. It was like whirling fireflies joining together in a stream flowing to the end of the universe. "They are going somewhere," I stated.

"What do you mean?"

"The lights, the buildings, the park and the people. They are moving toward eternity."

She smiled. "Arlo, you surprise me. I'm still not accustomed to your insights." She looked around the apartment. "Are you sure this belongs to you?"

"Yes, to me and my uncle, Louie."

"That's another surprise about you. Some weeks ago, I saw you as this lost kid with a stuffed suitcase sleeping with a blanket on the deck of a rusted boat. Now, this." She waved her hand around the room and toward the window and said, "Your parents must be wealthy."

"No, they are not."

"Then how did you get this, if I may ask?"

"Predicting horse races and stocks."

"Oh, come on Arlo. You're only thirteen. How's that possible?"

"It's what I do. I think and grow rich. And anyway, I'm almost fourteen."

Jill froze for a moment. "That's beyond my imagination."

"It isn't imagination. It's real."

"Arlo, that's scary, at least for a person like me."

"Yes," I said, understanding that I am different from others. I'd just have to accept that most other people are not normal like me.

"I have a question," Jill asked.

"Okay."

"I helped you get back to New York. We didn't talk about how long I should stay here or what I should be doing, but I will be starting university in September in the U.K., and I should go back to get a summer job."

"Would it be alright if I gave you a job?"

"Doing what?"

"To help me. When I don't have routines, I can become wobbly and disoriented, like when I'm in crowds. It's best if there's someone with me. Maria did that for me, but she died."

"But on the Ambrosia, you seemed to do just fine."

"That's because there weren't a lot of people and the routines every day were regular. Now, being back in New York it'll be different, and I need help. Could you work for me during the summer? I'll pay you."

"And what would I do for you?"

"Just be a help."

"A help?" She asked.

"Yes, go with me when I need to go places, do shopping and cooking if you want to, or we can go to restaurants. But it is better when things are simple."

"Let me think about it," she said.

"I will pay you whatever you make in your summer job in the U.K. and more."

She looked at me and then stared out the window at the lights below. She said, "This is my first time in New York. The view is stunning."

"There are many things to see, like Central Park and museums and Broadway shows and The New York Stock Exchange."

"The stock exchange?"

"Yes, that is the most interesting of everything."

She laughed. "Arlo, I'll take your offer, but at the end of summer I need to go back to the U.K. to start university."

CHAPTER 38

Jill stayed in one of our guest bedrooms. We had two of them, and she picked the one with the view toward the south.

The following morning after we arrived I woke up early, having that sensation Maria called jetlag.

An hour later Jill walked into the living room wearing a robe Louie had bought for guests. Jill was our first guest. Her long blond hair was wet, and when she walked by me, I smelled roses that filled the room.

There was nothing to eat in the kitchen, so Jill made coffee which we drank black. It was nothing like the black coffee they served in Greece.

Then I called Louie at the Hope Center.

"I'm back in New York," I said.

"Darn it, Arlo. You really make me nervous. It's been weeks since I last heard from you."

I wondered what it would be like to be nervous, as Louie experienced it. "Are you coming to the city?" I asked.

"I'll come this weekend. There are not many activities at the Hope Center on weekends."

"Can you help me with something, in a few weeks."

"And, what's that?" He asked.

"To go to the horse races."

He was quiet for a moment and then said, "Arlo, I ain't doing that no more. My life has changed."

"Please, just one time. For a particular reason."

"What's that?"

"I'll explain when we have more time together," I said. Even though Louie knew me better than anyone, it would be difficult to tell him that it had to be done because of the oak tree.

"Then we need to talk," he said, but I ain't going to no horse races. Anyway, there's something I need to tell you."

"What's that?"

"I met someone here at the Hope Center, a counselor. They're not supposed to get close to patients, but I got her to break the rules. You know me. We're now talking marriage."

That was unusual. "The day I fell out of the oak tree you told grandfather that marriage ain't for you."

Louie laughed. "You've got a good memory, but things have changed."

We hung up, and I thought about what he said. It was possible that marriage would be good for him, to help him get over the torment from Iwo Jima.

Jill and I went out for a late breakfast, and I saw cool greens and light blues when she was with me, similar colors as Maria. After breakfast, we walked in Central Park and then took a taxi to the Metropolitan Museum.

I had been to the museum several times before, and each time I couldn't go into too many rooms. Each painting was a colorful attack. Having visited the Louvre Museum, maybe I now had a higher tolerance level. With Jill, we visited quite a few rooms and most of the time I had to put my hand on her shoulder.

When we walked out of the museum, I said, "Tomorrow can you help me."

"Sure, that's what I'm here for."

"I need to go visit someone."

"And who is that?"

"His name is Al."

"Al?

"Yes, he works for an organization called the Mafia."

Her face froze and then she chuckled and said, "You're joking."

I replied, "No."

"The Mafia?"

"It's like a company only you can't find them listed on the New York Stock Exchange."

* * *

Jill and I took the elevator up to the third floor of the building where Al had his office. I put my hand on her shoulder because elevators made me wobbly. Then we walked to Al's office, and I turned the door handle and opened the door.

There was a shuffling noise as we went inside, and Al was seated behind his desk, reaching inside a drawer. He pulled out a handgun.

On one side of the room, a large man quickly stood up from a chair, and a gun was in his hand, and he pointed it at us. I recognized him and remembered that his name was Georgio.

I looked at Al and said, "I forgot to knock. Maria said I should do that."

"Whew," Al said. "You can't come in here like that."

Jill put her hand on my arm. Her eyes were round, and I saw jagged yellow emanating from her.

Al put the gun back on his desk, smiled and said, "You're that kid."

"I'm Arlo."

Georgio also smiled and said, "Hey kid. Give us that look, that Al look."

"I only do that when I want someone to do something for me when I think they don't want to. Maria taught me that."

Al kept looking at Jill and not at me. "Is that Maria," he asked.

"No, this is Jill."

"Wow, she's a looker."

"She looks at a lot of things," I said.

Georgio laughed, his stomach rolling up and down. "This kid is a real card."

They used new terms I didn't know, so needed to look them up in a dictionary.

"Why are you here?" Al asked.

"I'm looking for Mario Portalini, and the last time I was here, you said you knew him. How can I find him?"

"I wish I knew. He has a lot of my money, and I want it back."

"He has my money too. That's why I want to see him."

"Tell me again why he has your money?" Al asked.

"Because he took it when he left his bucket shop in Chicago."

Al was quiet for a second and then relaxed back in his chair. "Yeah, I know all about that. He was an absolute failure for what he was sent to do."

"Well, I need to see him," I stated.

"Mario disappeared about a week ago. If you find him, you tell him he better come and see me, or he will literally sink. We'll give him a pair of concrete boots and let him go for a walk in the Hudson River."

"He would drown," I stated.

"Smart kid. You get the point."

"What was he doing for you?" I asked.

"Some people loaned him money to start an investment office over by the stock exchange. Then he disappeared."

"You mean a bucket shop?"

"You call it what you want," Al said.

"What was the address?"

Al wrote out the address on a piece of paper and handed it to me. He said, "If you find Mario you tell him Al needs to talk with him."

"Thank you," I replied.

"Thank you? For what?" Al asked.

"Yes, Maria taught me to say that."

"Oh, my."

Behind Al, I saw two paths and a dark mitt was waiting on one of them. I said, "You have to be careful to make a choice. There is a black mitt that will hurt you if you stay here. Leave town, instead."

"Houston?"

I perceived he had been thinking of another place and now realized where it was, not only because he said it, but because of the brown, golden color, like oil on the dipstick of a motor.

Al looked at Georgio and then at me. "How do you know about Houston."

"I see the future in some people."

"But you couldn't have known about Houston."

"I did, because of the dipstick dripping around you?"

Al looked at Georgio and said, "This kid is nuts."

Georgio said, "Boss, you better listen to him. If you get capped, I get capped."

I said, "Thank you," and Jill and I left, knowing that *capped* was another word I needed to look up.

CHAPTER 39

Going down in the elevator I put my hand on Jill's shoulder, and I sensed her strength, yet fragility, like delicateness, like a dove.

She looked at me and said, "Arlo, what have you gotten me into?"

"The elevator?" I asked.

"No, not an elevator. Those men. Did you see those guns?"

"Yes. Both men had guns."

"And they could have shot us. Did you think about that?"

"Yes, but I knew they wouldn't."

"Oh goodness. How did you know that?"

"Because before we went in, I saw the dark mitt and knew that Al needed to make a choice. That was confirmed when I saw the golden-brown oil, although I didn't know that was connected to Houston."

"That for me is looney. If that happens again, I'm heading back to the U.K."

"It won't happen again, except maybe with Mario. We'll see."

We took a taxi to the address Al had given me, and Jill was silent all the way. From the light blue colors around her head, I knew she was thinking. That is something people do when they are stressed or when they must make a significant decision.

We went to Mario's bucket shop office, and it was locked, yet there was something about the place that gave me a forecast. From my time in New York, I knew this neighborhood, and I saw Mario's movement.

We walked out on the main street, and I followed a green stream several blocks, and then turned and went down a street with liquor stores, old theatres, run down restaurants and several cheap hotels.

In the past, I had seen Mafia type people going into a particular hotel. While the green stream split apart in different directions, I took the one to that single hotel. It felt like a guess that wasn't a guess.

I went inside, and Jill followed. An older man sat behind an open window, not quite like the booths at the race track, but similar. He looked at me and then at Jill and asked, "Do you need a room?"

"No. I'm looking for Mario. Mario Portalini."

"We don't have anyone here by that name," he claimed.

I saw a slimy color in his words, like swirling mix between apple green and Mikado yellow. I looked at the wall behind the man and then declared, "He's here."

"You calling me a liar?" He asked.

"Yes," I said, seeing guilt-orange in his words. "He is on the second floor."

"No, he isn't." He shifted back and forth in his chair.

I stated, "If you don't tell the truth, you will be kept out of the eternal city."

His upper lip turned up, and an eye squinted. "What-ah-ya talkin' about?" He asked.

"I can show you which room," I said.

The man peered at me and then at Jill. "Okay, he might still be here. Third floor, room three o' five."

We took a creaky elevator to the third floor, got out, and walked down a hallway until we came to Mario's room.

"This time knock," Jill said. "No more guns."

"Thank you," I said.

I knocked, and there wasn't an answer and then knocked again.

The door had one of those little round viewers where someone in a room could look outside. Through it, I saw movement.

"Mario, it's Arlo. I need to talk with you."

The door slowly opened. Mario showed half his face and said, "What in the world are you doing here."

"I came to talk with you.

"Ah, okay," he said.

He opened the door and motioned for us to come inside.

He looked at me as though he didn't recognize me. "Arlo, you've grown since Chicago. New York is a strange place for you to be, isn't it?"

"I'm not too sure what is strange."

"Who's your friend."

I had my hand on Jill's left shoulder, and I felt her tighten. She said, "That's none of your business."

Mario smiled and said, "Where'd you pick up this Limey babe?"

"What's a Limey?" I asked.

"He's uncouth," Jill stated.

Mario said, "Okay, okay. So, Arlo, what have you been up to?"

"Some travel."

"Why are you here?"

"I want my money."

He sat down in a chair that was between his bed and a well-worn wooden table with an old telephone on it. He looked at Jill and me with an Al kind of look and then asked, "What money?"

"From Chicago. F.E.S. Investments bucket shop. My account was emptied."

"Arlo, you cleaned me out. I've never seen anyone play the markets like you."

"I don't play markets."

"How do you have such an uncanny ability to guess price changes?"

"I see the future," I stated.

His face froze for a moment, and then he laughed. "That's a good one."

"No, really, I do."

"Come on, you're jiving me?"

"Uh, uh."

"Okay, tell me about my future."

"You're in trouble with some people, Al and Georgio, and their bosses. They're looking for you. Unless you do what I say, you'll be wearing concrete boots and walking at the bottom of the Hudson River."

His face froze. "How do you know these things?"

"Because I know the future. In Chicago you saw my abilities, so you better believe it now."

His face turned red, and he pounded his sizeable thick fist on the old table next to him. The telephone jumped in the air. It was an impressive movement. Jill's shoulders twitched.

He said, "Kid, I could break you in half."

For a moment I had an image of two separate halves of a body. I said, "I heard that expression before, but it never made logical sense. One can break a stick in half, but is it possible with the human body?"

"Huh?" He asked.

"To break a body into two pieces?"

"What-a-ya talking about? Come on. You know what I mean."

"I think so, but from the redness on your face and by hitting the table I believe that you have angry feelings."

"That's right. Kid, you kill me," he replied.

"The logic of your reaction should be different."

"Huh?"

"Fear is a better response."

"What are you talking about?"

"I wonder what it's like to wear concrete boots?"

Mario took a deep breath.

"Arlo, I'm in a bind. What should I do?"

"It's more than a *bind*. If you pay the money you owe me, then I can save you. It's nine hundred and ninety-nine thousand dollars. I could ask for interest, but round it up to one hundred thousand, and we're good."

"Hold on kid, where'd I get that kind of money."

"Look in the suitcase under your bed. It's there along with a lot more. It really belongs to Al, but I won't say anything to him because of how he threatened my uncle Louie."

"You're scary Arlo. How do you know about the money in the suitcase?"

The suitcase could be seen sticking out from under his bed. It was unlikely Mario put his money in banks, so he had to keep it somewhere, and he would want quick access to it. The suitcase was a logical deduction. I said, "Mario, I see things. If you want help, then I need my money. You owe it to me, and Al told me you should pay it."

He grinned. "Maybe I'll take my chances." With his left hand, he reached under the pillow on his bed, and he pulled out a handgun, and he placed it on the table.

Jill took a step backward.

I said, "I see what'll happen to you. If you want me to leave, I'll just say goodbye and good luck."

I gave him a small wave and then turned and headed for the door.

Before I reached the door, Mario cried out. "Wait. Kid, you've got to help me."

I turned around, and he bent down, pulled out the suitcase and opened it. He counted out ten bound bundles of dollar bills and said, "Here's your money."

"I don't have anything to put them in," I said.

He went to a cupboard and took out two large paper bags. I flipped through the bundles, and they all contained hundred-dollar bills.

Taking the paper bags, I filled them with the dollars.

"So, what should I do?" He asked.

Having thought about this before we got to his room, I said, "Today, take the afternoon flight to Paris. From there take a train to Genoa in Italy."

Mario's large body leaned toward me. "To Italy?"

I said, "There's a travel agency in Genoa, and you need to talk with Annetta Allegra. She can help people disappear to anywhere. Do you have something I can write on?"

Mario took a pencil from the drawer of the table, dug out a piece of paper from his trash can, and gave them to me. Then I wrote down the address of Annetta's agency and handed it to him.

"This is nuts," he said.

"Not really. It concerns your well-being. It's better than concrete boots."

"Absolutely nuts," he stated.

"Al and Georgio are coming here today. Call them if you don't believe me."

He looked at the telephone on the old table, but his hand didn't move. "How do you know these things?"

"I told you, I see the future. I've had this ability since the day I fell out of an oak tree, but it was on Patmos that I understood more of it."

"What are you talking about?" He asked.

"Read John's book, and you will understand."

"Who?"

Jill spoke up. "Patmos, you dummy. It's where John wrote the Book of Revelation. Maybe, if you read it, you won't be so barmy."

"Huh, barmy?" He asked.

"Barmy. British, for a stupid idiot," she stated.

He stared at her with wide eyes like he suffered from the shock of being transported to another world.

I said, "I'll call Annetta and tell her that you're coming. She can help you disappear."

After handing one of the paper bags to Jill, I took the other, and then we left Mario's room.

Before closing the door, I saw him in the chair, leaning forward with his elbows on his knees and his hands holding his head.

When we waited for the elevator, I turned around and looked at the door to Mario's room.

Hovering in the background was my oak tree, and it sighed relief as a big ominous bird lifted from a branch and flew away. But, there were more weights on the tree.

CHAPTER 40

Once we left the building, Jill declared, "This is absolutely bonkers."

"Bonkers?" I asked.

"Oh Arlo, I need to teach you to speak proper English."

"You use some words that I don't know, especially the ones from England."

"What did they teach you in school?" She asked.

"I never went to school except for a few days each year, mostly learning from reading the newspapers."

"As I said, this is totally bonkers."

"Why is that?"

"Think about it. Do you honestly believe that I go around every day facing thugs with guns?"

"If you tell me what you do every day, then I can answer that question."

"Unequivocally bonkers. In this paper bag is more money than I've ever seen in my life. Did you see the way you took it from that guy?"

"You mean with my hands?"

"No, I mean the way you spoke to him. Don't you have any fear of these people."

"Fear might be black rivers, but there wasn't any. Anyway, why shouldn't they fear me?"

Her neck was red, and I had difficulty to know if that was because of distress or anger. It most likely was not due to embarrassment. I wished Maria was here to help me interpret this body language.

Jill declared, "If this continues, I'm going back to the U.K."

"There are consequences if you do that," I said.

She stared at me and asked, "How did you know Mario was in that hotel and in that room? Did you actually find him through telepathy or clairvoyance, or something like that?"

"I don't know what those things are. It was only a calculated guess what hotel he was in. If he wasn't there, then we could have gone to others. Then on the wall behind the receptionist, there was a rack with room keys. All the hooks had keys except for room three zero five. It was just logic."

"So, you were guessing and not really seeing where Mario was in some spooky way."

"Guessing yes, but the slimy apple green and Mikado yellow coming out of the receptionist told me he was lying, and that Mario was there."

"Slimy apple green. I certainly didn't see that," Jill stated.

"And Mikado yellow."

"Oh goodness, this is beyond bonkers."

We didn't discourse much after that but took a taxi back to my apartment.

* * *

On Friday afternoon Louie showed up at the apartment. He walked in, shook my hand man to man, and then gave me a powerful hug. I realized that I was slightly taller than him.

As we talked, I saw something different about him. He was relaxed, and the dark cloud of Iwo Jima drifted far in the background.

Jill was getting groceries, so Louie and I had time to talk. We sat down in the living room.

He said, "I'm glad you're back. I worried about you but was deep in my own head. The Hope Center's been good for me."

There was something I was curious about. "You said you were talking about getting married. Who is she?" I asked.

"Her name is Sue, and she is something special."

Louie's words were baby blue, and there was a white

atmosphere around him, not like the dark one he had carried in the past.

"And you Arlo, how are you?"

He had never asked me that before. "I am normal," I said.

He laughed. "That you are. I mean, what have you been doing?"

He knew about London, Maria and Spain, and Patmos because I had told him on the telephone. So, I told him about my events in New York with Al and Mario.

Louie grumbled, "That's enough. Don't go around Al anymore."

"I won't. I think Al and Georgio will move to Houston."

"That's good." He paused. "Tell me about this Jill. How does she fit in?"

I said, "Colors are more balanced when someone helps me. Jill gives composed colors. When I get wobbly, she provides stability, like Maria."

He nodded his head, and I noticed his movement was similar to that of my grandfather. "Yes, it's better when you have someone."

The apartment door opened, and Jill came in carrying a bag of groceries. I introduced her to Louie, and she went into the kitchen.

Louie said, "Man, she's beautiful."

"It's true. Most of the time Jill is surrounded by satin whites and soft pastels, but sometimes a crimson fire can come from her, like when we met Mario, and she called him barmy."

Louie laughed, but I wasn't sure what was funny.

He said, "Perhaps your criteria of beauty are superior to that used by the rest of us."

Jill joined us, and after a time of chit-chat, I said, "Louie, Can I ask your help?"

"Anything you want," he responded.

"In two weeks would you go with me somewhere, to Elmont."

"Why is that?"

"It's the Belmont Stakes."

He smiled. "Arlo, I told you on the phone that I ain't doing that no more."

"I understand, but Maria said not to say *ain't*."

"Okay, I got it," he said. "I'm not going to racetracks anymore."

"Please, I need your help only this one time."

"How's that?" He asked.

"I can't tell you now, but I'd like you to take me there, and for Jill to come."

He took a deep breath and put his hand on the back of his head, and that movement was exactly like when he touched his head after being clubbed by the robbers. The colors from this told me that he was thinking about that event.

Louie said, "Okay, I'll do it for you."

CHAPTER 41

It was June 7th, 1958, a hot New York day at the Belmont Racetrack. The heat didn't bother me as much as the large crowd of over thirty thousand people.

Louie, Jill and I entered the racetrack, and I supported myself on Louie's shoulder, just like the old times.

The first race had not started, and I said to Louie, "Let's find Snodgrass and Minx."

His face became something like a dried-out orange. He said, "I want nothing to do with those two guys after what they did to us a year ago."

"Don't worry," I said. "I have a plan."

"What is it?" He demanded.

I whispered, "It is for justice. You'll understand during the day."

"You sure about this?"

"Yes, I can see the future."

Jill turned to me and said, "I told you I don't want any more brutes with guns."

I reached over and took her hand, which Maria said was a reassuring gesture. "Don't worry, these guys are not in the Mafia corporation, and they don't have guns. They only work with men with clubs They need help."

Louie grinned. "Arlo, you surprise me. What shall we do?"

"We can find them at the betting booths, but whatever you do, stay friendly."

"With those guys? No way."

"You must do what I say. Don't get angry with them."

We made our way to the betting booths where men lined up ready to place their bets. Snodgrass and Minx were at the end of a line, so we went in behind them.

They didn't notice us, so I tapped Snodgrass on the shoulder. As he turned around, I stared at the ground.

Snodgrass seemed startled to see us, but then he smiled a smile that wasn't a smile. "Ah, Louie. What are you doing here?"

"Same as you. This is the big day, last race of the Triple Crown."

By that point, Minx was looking at me, and he said to Louie, "I see you still have the nitwit with you, and who's the sweetheart?"

Jill glared at him.

Louie said, "He's not a nitwit. You'll see."

I was worried that Louie might become angry and even get into a fight, convinced he could easily beat them to a pulp. That was an expression I understood for when they made paper they beat the wood to a pulp.

I said, "Chance-John will win the first race."

Minx laughed and said, "No way. They gave that horse the wrong name. He should be called, Not A Chance in Hell."

"Careful how you talk around the kid," Louie stated. You should listen to him."

"We'll stick with our pick," Snodgrass said.

We bought our ticket, and Chance-John won the race, paying fifteen to one. The horse that Snodgrass and Minx had chosen came in third place.

At the beginning of the next four races, I told Snodgrass and Minx the names of the horses that would win. Before the sixth race, they came to us, and Snodgrass asked, "What's with this kid? He guesses everything correctly."

Louie smiled. "He's a horse prophet. He's not good for much, but show him a racing form, and he gets it right a hundred percent of the time."

Snodgrass looked at me and asked, "So, who's going to win the next race?"

"I know," I stated while staring at the ground.

"Which horse?"

"I'm not telling you."

"Come on kid. You can tell us."

"Okay, it's Surplus."

Snodgrass said, "I would never have guessed."

"Put all your money on Surplus, and you'll see."

"We don't ever put all our money on one horse," Minx said. "It's good risk management."

My eyes shifted from staring at the ground to staring into his eyes, and I said, "We're putting all our money on Surplus." Then I turned to Louie and asked, "How much money do we have now?"

Louie reached patted his front right pants pocket and said, "Seven thousand dollars."

"And you're betting all of that on Surplus?" Minx asked.

Louie nodded and said, "For sure, all of it. The kid gets it right all the time."

Minx looked at Snodgrass who nodded.

Snodgrass said, "We'll bet a thousand on the horse."

Surplus won the race, and it paid three to one. The next race was the Belmont Stakes where the best horses in the world competed for a large prize.

Louie and I went to the betting booths, and Snodgrass and Minx rushed up to us.

Minx said, "It was unbelievable. So, who's going to win the Stakes?"

"I won't tell you," I said.

"Kid, you've got to. Please tell us," Minx said.

I looked at the ground and then up and then right and left and then back to the ground again. I slowly put my hand on Louie's shoulder and leaned against him, then looked up and then at the ground again.

"You're killing us," Snodgrass said.

"It will be Page Seven," I stated.

"Page Seven?" Snodgrass said. "The odds are eighty-nine to one on that horse."

"I know. We are putting everything we own on that horse, twenty-one thousand dollars."

In looking at the faces of Snodgrass and Minx, I recognized the look of greed, as Maria had taught me, which also had a color. They glanced at each other, and Minx asked Snodgrass, "Shall we? Everything?"

Snodgrass nodded and stated, "Everything."

"That's thirty thousand dollars, our entire fortune," Minx said.

Snodgrass nodded again. "With odds of eighty-nine to one, that's over, two and a half million for us. The kid never gets it wrong."

"We were behind them in the line, and when they got to the betting booth, I heard Minx say, "Thirty thousand on Page Seven."

Snodgrass took the ticket, put it in his pocket and they charged off to the stands."

When we reached the booth, Louie turned to me and said, "How much should we put on Page Seven?"

I spoke with a soft voice. "Nothing. Put all our winnings from the previous races on Cavan."

Louie looked at me and laughed like his cheeks would break. He said, "You never cease to amaze me."

We didn't go up to the stands to see the race but stayed in front of the betting booth. The announcer described the action over the loudspeaker.

Page Seven came in last, far last. Cavan paid four to one, which for us was our bet of twenty-one thousand times four.

We got our winnings of eighty-four thousand dollars and headed straight to our red Ford Fairlane convertible, knowing that Snodgrass and Minx would search for us. This time I put my hand on Jill's shoulder.

As we drove away from the racetrack, Louie laughed and said, "That was crazy fun, and I enjoyed every second of it, but I don't want to do it anymore."

"I know. This was the last time, but justice was needed, and more justice is coming."

"What are you talking about?" Jill asked.

"A final day of judgment is coming for every person, but there are life judgments before the final one. Snodgrass and Minx wronged us a year ago. It might redeem them if they see how it feels."

"Where did you learn this?" Louie asked.

"On John's island, Patmos, when I read his book."

CHAPTER 42

When I considered Snodgrass, I saw fresh greens and blues, knowing a river would soon lead him away from racetracks and into a job in his hometown in Indiana. Minx's life was a river of red flowing over rocks, choppy and turbulent, disappearing over a waterfall.

Seeing the future of those men made me try and look at my own destiny, but it was translucent and difficult to perceive. All I knew was that another weight had been taken off the oak tree and now it was able to breathe and bend with the wind.

But, there were still other forces pushing down on the tree, and I knew I needed to deal with them. Otherwise, the oak tree would always be a restriction on me.

As Louie drove back to the apartment, he laughed most of the way. At one point he said, "Nephew, I didn't know you had it in you. What you did to those two clowns was well deserved."

"And, I'm glad they didn't have guns," Jill stated.

I said, "They needed justice, and it was done to help Snodgrass. Life will change for him."

Louie quickly glanced at me and pointed his eyes back to the road. He asked, "How did you come up with that?"

"On Patmos."

"You mean you can guess the outcome of people like guessing cars and horses and the stock market?"

"Something like that, but not all the time. It's more complicated because people make choices and the alternatives are varied. Though, at the same time, no matter what the options, history is flowing to an end."

"How do you know this?"

"On Patmos, I read John's book about how he saw the world and the future. It is full of amazing images, and they make sense of how everything fits together."

"Fits together?"

"Yeah, you know how when you read in the newspapers about how things happened? John's book puts a perspective on that and how everything extends forward."

"And from that, you see the outcomes in people's lives?" Louie asked.

"Not a lot, but some."

We stopped at a red light, and he was quiet for a moment, and then he asked, "What do you see with me?"

The red light swirled toward us and engulfed him like it was suffocating him. Then the light turned green and the pressure lifted.

As Louie put his foot on the accelerator, I said, "What you experienced was not easy, the war and all of that. It hurt you and stopped you from being free. Meeting Sue is right for you. She will bring you good and not evil all the days of your life."

Louie smiled. "That's vague. Specifically, do you have any premonitions about my life?"

"Yes, you have choices that can lead in different directions."

"So, what are they?" He asked.

When we were alone, without Jill, I told him.

* * *

A week later Jill and I flew to San Diego. It was helpful to have her, as I didn't need to talk with people when buying airplane tickets or renting a car.

Jill was eighteen years old and was not an experienced driver. It took some time for the car rental agency to figure out her British driver's license, but they were happy to accept my traveler's cheques. At first, she had difficulty to drive, "On the wrong side of the road," as she put it. But she learned quickly.

We went to a town inland from San Diego called El Cajon. It was a hot, dry day, and the temperature reminded me of Patmos.

Jill drove into a housing development where the small houses all seemed to be of the same design, perhaps two or three bedrooms, each house painted a different pastel color. The paint was faded, and landscaping consisted of brownish-green lawns, gravel or hard packed dirt

I had an address of where we were going and a map of the area. Once we found the street and the house I was interested in, Jill parked the car. Just as she turned off the motor, a school bus stopped down the road. Children got out and scattered toward the different homes.

We sat in the car and watched.

Two kids walked toward the house we were watching. There was a girl, maybe six or seven years old and a boy, maybe five or six. The boy walked with a slight limp.

As they approached the house, the front door opened, and a woman emerged. She hugged them, first the girl and then the boy. She kissed the boy on his forehead.

The woman was slender and had light brown hair bordering on blond. She was seventeen years older than me and therefore was thirty years old.

"Is that her?" Jill asked.

"Yes. I replied. That's my mother."

"How do you feel?"

Jill's question was unanswerable for feelings were not something I knew. Instead, I saw yellow flowers encompassing the house. "I'll go talk to her," I said.

"Are you sure you want to do this?"

I had explained to Jill how I had not seen my mother since I was five years old. "Yes, I need to free the oak tree."

"What are you talking about?"

It would take too long to explain it to her, so I opened the door of the car, stepped out and walked to the house. My mother and the two children had gone inside.

The odor of oil rose up from the hot asphalt road, with a whiff of eucalyptus mixed in, because on one side of the street there was a eucalyptus forest.

These smells intermingled with the heat of the day becoming a gray-green cloud that pushed me forward. It was like they commanded me to fulfill a purpose.

I walked up the driveway to the garage and then turned onto a cracked concrete path to the front door. The doorbell button didn't work when I pushed on it, so I knocked four times.

When my mother opened the door, I gave her one of the smiles that Maria had taught me. "Hello mother," I said.

She looked at me, and her face froze, and then it quickly turned red, her eyes becoming watery. She was feeling emotion.

The emotion transformed into a moan coming deep from her insides. She put her hand against the doorframe for it looked like her legs were ready to collapse.

She tried to talk, and a few sounds emerged from her throat, and with short breaths, she said, "You look so much like him?"

"Like who?" I asked.

"Like your father."

Then she began to weep, and she buckled to her knees and grabbed my hand and started to cry while trying to say something that I eventually understood as, "I'm so sorry."

"Sorry for what?" I asked.

"I'm, I'm... I'm sorry for leaving you and for emptying your bank account. Guilts... Guilts I carry every single day. I'm so ashamed."

I had learned about guilt. It was a feeling people had when they understood they had done something wrong and they felt sorry for it.

This was an unusual situation, and I wasn't sure if there was more to say, so I said, "I should go now."

I tried to remove her hand from mine, but she held on.

"No, wait. Please don't go," she pleaded.

She was experiencing deep emotion, and I couldn't get a fix on it. Instead, when she spoke, I saw the stream of her words like a tangled woodpile that needed to be orderly stacked.

And I understood that I was the one who should stack the woodpile.

"I can help you," I said.

When I said that, it was like she couldn't produce words. She exhaled a moan and tears rolled down her face. With a weak voice, she said, "Arlo, you don't know what you say. I have hurt you, and I don't see how you could help."

I searched inside myself to understand how she had hurt me. I think she meant emotionally rather than physically. Whatever she had done, which I didn't fully grasp, I was fixed on stacking the woodpile, and once I get a goal, I can't let go of it. She didn't know it, but the goal had been set in Patmos, and she was a part of it. "There are problems to be fixed," I stated. "Please get up."

I pulled her up by one hand, and with her other hand, she supported herself against the doorframe.

After taking a few breaths, she said, "Come inside."

"May I bring my friend?"

"Your friend?"

"My driver in the car over there, my helper and friend. She is important for my future."

My mother looked across the street where Jill was sitting in the car, and she waived at Jill and motioned for her to come.

Jill got out of the car and walked across the street and introduced herself.

My mother said, "Are you from England?"

"Yes."

"How in the world did you meet Arlo?"

"On a tramp-steamer called the Ambrosia in the Greek islands."

My mother had no response. She stood for a while looking at us and then said, "Please come in."

CHAPTER 43

Jill and I sat on a long couch like the one at my grandfather's house, worn in places and with spots. The pink flowers in the design were faded.

My mother sat across from us in an armchair. She said, "I'm at a loss for words. You don't know how many times I wanted to go to you, but my husband prohibited me from doing so. Then life got complicated, especially last year."

The sound of the children laughing came from one of the rooms down a hallway.

Jill asked, "Why would your husband forbid you?"

"He knew Arlo's, ah... condition. My husband didn't want to take on that responsibility." She looked down at her folded hands. "He was a hard man."

Jill hesitated for a moment and then said, "Excuse me for asking, but you used the word *was*."

The sound of Jill's voice was interesting to me how each syllable came out distinct. For instance, when she said the word water you could hear a distinct 't' in it, not like when we said it in the United States, which was more like a 'd', like *wader*.

My mother said, "Last year my husband was driving too fast and crashed his car and... and was killed. My son Jimmy was gravely injured and is still not fully recovered."

"I'm so sorry to hear that," Jill replied.

Tears came to my mother's eyes. "Arlo, I should never have listened to that wicked man. Before I met him, life was so hard, having lost my husband, your father, in the war. I was an emotional wreck being so young and with a child to care for. And, I don't know how to say it, but you were not easy."

"Don't worry," I replied. "My teachers said the same thing to my grandfather and Uncle Louie."

She continued. "Even so, I should have made different choices. You must understand that a smooth-talking man came along, we were married, and then he became extremely controlling and violent. I lived in constant fear from his abuse, and I was too weak to free myself from him. When you were with us, he constantly demanded that I get rid of you, and I was afraid that he would harm you. Finally, I gave in and drove you to your grandfather's farm."

"I remember your Pontiac, light blue, 1947," I said.

"That's remarkable," she said. "You were so young. That day I was so distraught when I left you with your grandfather. I felt so much pain and guilt after that. The memory that has stayed with me is of this small blue-eyed boy with a lonely look on his face, watching as I drove away."

"It's okay," I said, thinking that's what I was supposed to say. I mostly remembered the sound of the engine of her car.

"When I got back to San Diego, my husband didn't allow me to drive the car again because he didn't want me to go back and see you. Eventually, I gave in to him."

"You had difficult times," I remarked, remembering how Maria taught me to show empathy.

"How can you be so nice to me after what I've done, especially taking the money from your bank account. You see, I had costly medical bills after the car crash when Jimmy was somewhere between life and death. And, it took weeks for him to recover in the hospital."

That caught my attention, for my mother said, 'in the hospital' whereas, with British English, Jill would say "in hospital."

My mother continued. "There was something else besides the hospital bills. My husband owed a lot of money because of gambling debts. After the car crash, my husband's bookie threatened to take away our house, even making death threats to my children. I was desperate."

"You shouldn't gamble," I stated.

"I know. It was an addiction with him, and he didn't listen to reason, and he got way in over his head."

"Gamblers do that," I said, thinking about Louie and Snodgrass and Minx and Al and Georgio.

"But, what about the money I took from you, seventy-five thousand dollars? How can I pay it back?"

"I won it at the horse races and other ways," I replied.

My mother said, "But you just told me you shouldn't gamble."

"I don't gamble,"

"I don't understand. How can I pay you back?"

"Oh, I didn't come here for that," I stated. "The money doesn't matter. Money is just a way to help for learning about life. For instance, I learned that one needs to build protections and be wise for things like this, and for avoiding people like Mario."

"Who is Mario," my mother asked.

"He was a buzzard, a bucket-shop owner in Chicago, but now he is in Italy trying to escape something called the Mafia."

"I'm sorry Arlo, but I'm confused," my mother said. "Why did you come here?"

"Because I perceived that your river was turbulent, and it evaporated in a dry desert. Then that was confirmed when you spoke, and I saw the tangled woodpile that needed straightening and then there is the weight on the oak tree."

"That's even more confusing," she said.

My mother needed enlightenment. "You need to read John's book from the island of Patmos."

"Where?"

"Patmos in Greece."

My mother said, "Arlo, you're only thirteen years old. Where have you been?"

"I was fourteen two days ago on June 12th. A week ago, on June 7th, we were at the Elmont Racetrack in New York watching The Belmont Stakes. Exactly one year ago on June 14th, Louie and I drove across America, and I was watching the clouds and horizon of Kansas from the back seat of our new Ford Fairlane convertible."

I wondered if I had adequately answered her question on where I had been.

"It is incredible for me to believe that you have been across America and to Europe. I'm glad. Again, I am so sorry for what has happened and for what I've done. Can you ever forgive me?"

"You fell into bad circumstances," I told my mother. A dark mist had been above her head, but now it was gone, and I saw a shattered vase that was in the process of being put back together. But, to be made perfectly whole, it would take time. "I have nothing to hold against you. The death of my father was hard on you and it has been hard ever since. We can get through this."

A tear rolled down her cheek and I also saw a watery mist in Jill's eyes. Then, I heard the noise of the children in the bedroom and thought it would be interesting to look at them up closely. "Can I meet my sister and brother?"

CHAPTER 44

Another weight was gone. When we left my mother's house, Jill encouraged me to think about taking care of my mother and brother and sister. That connected with something that Maria had said, that you could do good deeds with money. But, I needed someone to reveal what they were. Jill might be capable of that. Based on her perspective of the needs of my family, I agreed to regularly send money to them.

Now, one task remained. For this, we needed to go to our orange farm.

While driving back to the San Diego airport, I started thinking that we shouldn't fly to Los Angeles, but instead, go by car. And, it seemed logical that Jill should have her own car, one that was easy to operate.

We passed a car dealership, and I saw a red car that seemed ideal for her, so instructed her to turn around and pull into a car sales lot.

The car I had in mind seemed smaller than full-sized cars. Jill knew how to drive a stick shift, as there were few cars with automatic transmissions in England.

We spoke with a car salesman and then sat in the car. Then I asked the car salesman if I could use his phone to call my banker. I spoke with Grant Adams, and then he talked with the salesman and after signing some papers we drove away in a new 1958 Corvette. Corvettes are made by Chevrolet so Louie would be angry when he heard about this. But, my grandfather would have been proud.

The salesman said he would return the rental car.

On the drive up the coast to our orange farm, Jill kept saying, "This is crazy, absolutely bonkers. One week I'm in Patmos, and a few weeks later I'm in California driving on the wrong side of the road in a sports-car with the top down. And, the car is in my name. Absolutely bonkers."

"It's not crazy," I said. "It's a logical progression of events. I'm too young to own a car."

She took a deep breath and then spoke softly, so much so that I almost couldn't hear her because of the sounds of the traffic. "Whatever it is," she said, "I'm grateful that you got me away from Hugh."

"You're welcome," I said.

She drove a while without saying anything, and then said, "You know in a month my time is finished here, and I'll be heading back to England to start university."

I looked to our left and saw the expanse of the Pacific Ocean with large waves crashing toward the shore and then thought about Jill and what she was planning. Each person makes their own choices, their own history. Once choices are made, a person can't choose the consequences of their decisions.

My gaze drifted from the ocean to her. She wore a scarf over her head, and loose strands of blond hair blew in the wind. It reminded me of the horses I saw at racetracks as they thundered down the track to reach a destination. We were like that only thundering along a freeway.

And then I had a realization. Jill's destiny unfolded as sweeping rivers, or rather two possible directions leading to vastly different histories.

Without any warning, I proclaimed, "You have two main choices. Each has lots of little choices and little navigations."

She laughed. "Here we go again. So, what are they?"

"You can go back to England and become a nurse and work in a hospital. With that one there are more people like Hugh along your path."

"You mean I will fall for the same kind of man?"

"Yes, with many hurts along the way."

She was quiet and then said, "I see that. What's the other choice?"

"You can stay here to go to university to become a doctor, to help people, and to help me. That way you'll do interesting things, and there won't be hurts."

She glanced at me and then focused back on the road in front of us, and said, "Wow. That's blunt and to the point. Does that mean I can't become an artist or a banker?"

"Yes, you can. I'm just telling you about the two main paths that are logically in front of you."

She shook her head. "Since meeting you, it has been a wild ride, the craziest time of my life."

There was that word *wild* again like Louie had used it. Only, I didn't fully grasp what was so wild. "So, what's your choice?" I asked.

"I need to think about it."

* * *

From then on, we didn't talk much, for the blue-green hues above Jill indicated she was thinking.

The bright blue sea was on our left, and it was a similar color as Jill's eyes. The wind whistled above our heads and sunshine beat down on us. I wished I had my sailor's hat from Greece.

My focus was mostly on the last task on my list, perhaps the most important, but I also thought about what had been accomplished. First, I got my money back from Mario and saved him from having to wear concrete boots.

Second, Snodgrass would go to Indiana, whereas Minx would go over a waterfall. Third, I met my mother and thought I'd help her with her life, although Jill seemed better at helping people than me. Maria would have been happy about that.

And, then there was Al and Georgio who had most likely gone to Houston.

Another accomplishment was that Louie and I had won some

money during our very last time at the race track. That would help him get started in his new marriage. I had told him my idea about what he should do with his life, and he liked it.

The image of the oak tree followed me throughout my travels, and now it was changing. The tree had been untouchable, sending warning signals, yet it had tentacles that reached into every area of my life. Finding solutions for Mario and Snodgrass and my mother reduced the pressure from the tentacles and the weights they imposed.

Several miles away from the orange farm I noticed that some of the farms and orange trees around us were gone. Open areas had become construction sites with homes being built.

Several farms near ours had 'For Sale' signs in their front driveways. Houses would be built on them.

The heat of July was an illustration of what was to come, like the suffocating crowds of people moving in. Soon they would push right up to the edge of our property.

Jill drove the car into the short dirt driveway in front of our house and then turned off the engine. The porch gave memories of grandfather, and Louie and me sitting there each evening and guessing cars.

Carlos appeared from the orange groves, and he had a similar smile that I had practiced with Maria, but she said I never got it right.

Our house looked the same, but different. It was because I noticed details that had been invisible in the past. The blue paint on the side boards was peeling off. My grandfather's junkyard next to the house seemed to have more rust. It was probably like that before, but I hadn't noticed it. It's amazing how you can see familiar things in a new way when you look at them in detail or look at them with a fresh perspective. When you go away for a while and then come back, things change.

Soft swirls of light blue and green met me, and the familiarity of the place was like a protective bubble.

I took Jill inside, and it appeared more orderly than before. Carlos had cleaned it. Still, the floors and furniture were worn.

"This is where you live?" Jill asked.

"Since I was five years old when my mother left me here."

"I must say it is quite different than Bournemouth."

"I've never been to Bournemouth."

"I know."

"Someday I will go," I said.

"And maybe you will visit me there," she commented, "unless I accept your hair-brained scheme to stay in California."

"I didn't say California. I said here, meaning with me wherever I go."

"Universities don't move with people. They are in places."

"I know that. There is no conflict with the history."

"Arlo, that's not understandable."

"It is. And remember if you go back to England and become a nurse, you will face other problems like Hugh, and your life will have sadness."

"How do you know this?"

"I told you. I see the future."

"So, it's better to stay here in this rather, ah... primitive place?"

"Not here. You will go to university like I said but in New York. Our apartment is better for that. There, you are close to universities, and I am close to the stock market. And, I want to go to acting school. Then, I need someone to help me do many things in the world, and I want it to be you. You understand me, kind of like Maria did."

The idea from Napoleon Hill to think and grow rich still held logic for someone limited, like me, but something had pushed it down on my priority list. John's book gave a new perspective, one that was much broader and more far-reaching. It would be my guide in the years to come.

"I'm still not sure who this Maria is," Jill stated. "But, you may be right about going back to the U.K. I'd probably fall in with another loser like Hugh."

"It's not probable," I stated. "I'm trying to scare you with the truth to save you."

"Then I need to think seriously about this."

"Yes, you do."

* * *

I showed Jill around our farm, and we walked along the small path I'd run on so many times. The tug of an invisible rope pulled me to the oak tree, and I sensed an urge to run the path from the house to the tree. I resisted it. There was a final task to accomplish in order to be free.

When we reached the oak tree, I asked Jill to go back to the house and wait for me. She turned and disappeared down the path.

I stood looking at the oak tree, at the rough brown and black bark. It was all so familiar for I had memorized the shapes of each piece and the contours and the cracks between them.

The tree still sent electrical impulses, yellows, and reds, like I couldn't touch them, their tentacles extruding from the tree, pushing me away.

I thought of John's book, about how in the kingdom of silver and light there is a tree that is for the healing of the nations. The oak tree was insignificant in comparison to that tree.

Still, my body was filled with electricity when I forced my hand to touch the trunk of the tree.

And then I knew what I needed to do, to accomplish a task I had tried and failed.

But, I wasn't sure I could do it. The oak tree made my wobbly legs tremble.

CHAPTER 45

I am now ninety years old, and I know the day of my death. It will be at the end of September thirteen years from now. If you've done the math, I'll be one hundred and three years old.

There's one thing that could annul this prediction. The incredible being on the throne is coming back to judge the living and the dead, but no one knows the day or hour. We only know the signs of the times, and they are all in place. The exact day he comes is his decision alone.

I see the future, not all of it, but enough. During my life, I used this knowledge to achieve goals. One of them was to think and grow rich, but only rich enough to accomplish what was needed.

When you have special abilities, you don't realize they are unique, because you think they are normal for everyone. In today's world, they'd call me a *special needs person*. When I was young, they packaged a lot of human conditions into the terms *crippled* and *spastic* and *handicapped*.

In 1958, MRI and CT scan technology were in its infancy, but years later Jill took me to the New York and Presbyterian Hospital where they did a scan of my brain. That's where she did her medical studies.

When the results were ready, Jill and I went to the hospital where we met with a top medical professor. We waited for him in his office, and I read the diplomas on one of his walls. I had never made it out of grade school.

The professor walked into his office, shook our hands and then sat behind his desk. He opened a manila folder containing the results of my scan.

He said, "Mr. Harkin, the scan gave us interesting results. From a medical point of view we observe something unique, which is of interest to the medical community, and I don't in any way want to alarm you in disclosing the results but clinically we have not seen many cases like this, and as I said, there is nothing to cause alarm, but it is quite remarkable, of significant medical interest."

I interjected, "Doctor Green, you can be direct. What are the results?" His words were like yellow and gray fog, and he was avoiding specifics. Whatever the results I wouldn't feel alarmed. If anything, I would be fascinated.

He looked at me and then at Jill and then back at me. He peered again at the papers and said, "I'm surprised that you are able to function normally."

"Why is that?" I asked.

"Your motor skills are functional, whereas your brain scan shows anomalies."

Jill looked at him and said, "Professor Green, as Arlo said, you can be straightforward with us. I've been in your classes in medical school, and Arlo and I like to work with the facts.

Dr. Green smiled and said, "Yes Jill, I remember you as a student as well as your honest approach to science and medicine."

"I think I was more like a pain," she stated.

"Not really. I appreciate students who challenge existing paradigms."

"We are waiting for the results," I said.

He adjusted his glasses looked at the papers in front of him and said, "Most people with your condition would be limited in their verbal or motor skills, or in their cognitive abilities. And, their social skills would be lacking."

Little did he know that I had to work hard to achieve what was perceived to be average social skills. The classes at the New York School of Acting had helped, and my expressions and timing improved. Although, I never got it perfect. You could say they'd never put me in the movies.

Whatever Dr. Green perceived in me as normal, was in fact, acting. The experience of acting school also made me question how many other people are acting out something they really are not? "What's wrong?" I asked.

"There are two main anomalies. First, you have a condition called partial ACC or agenesis of the corpus callosum."

Jill turned to me and said, "Arlo, that's where the two hemispheres of the brain are partially connected. It's a rare congenital disorder in which the brain typically develops irregularly during pregnancy."

"How serious is it?" I asked.

Dr. Green replied, "This condition is usually quite debilitating."

"And, what's the second anomaly?" I asked.

"There is damage to the left anterior temporal lobe, an area of the brain key in processing sensory input. Some autistic people have this injury. One outcome is that emotions can be processed abnormally. Do you remember having an accident when you were a child?"

I smiled and said, "I fell out of a tree."

"And have you experienced any extraordinary sensations or abilities from this?" He asked.

"Maybe sometimes I'm able to guess things. Why do you ask?" I didn't want to tell the doctor an untruth.

"There are few people with your condition, and about ten percent of those have special abilities, like memorizing books or being able to calculate complex formulas. It's called savant syndrome. Some can hear a piece of classical music one time and then they can play it. Others have exceptional artistic abilities."

"I wish I could do that," I stated.

"Synesthesia can also be an outcome." He said.

"I think I'm just an average guy," I claimed. That wasn't a lie, for I figured I was normal in my own way. And, I already knew what synesthesia was. It is when you perceive sensory input in colors or smells. For instance, it was how I saw the words of people in colorful bubbles, streams and spaghetti strands.

He nodded his head. "You are lucky. Most people with your pathology need special care."

I had special care. I had Jill.

Getting the results of that exam from Dr. Green was a revelation, and it captured my thinking for days after we left his office. It explained the cause of my uniqueness, but did it explain why I had an extraordinary ability to see the future? Having read John's book, I always wondered if this ability came from a different source. Did it come directly from the divine, the one on the throne?

The only conclusion was that my physical and mental condition and my unique abilities were a special gift.

* * *

I am ninety years old, and I stand by the window of our apartment and look out at the city in front of us. There are more tall buildings than when we first moved here in the late 1950's.

The world has changed, and I predicted those changes. I no longer get dizzy when I see that view, for I now comprehend what is beyond it.

I use my cane for support and shuffle into Jill's room, and she sits up on her bed and is writing something on a yellow legal pad. Her face is wrinkled, and her hair is now gray. The same blue-green hue emanates from her as when I first met her. I also see distinctive pastels and pinks.

She is ninety-five years old.

She smiles when she sees me and puts the legal pad next to her on the bed.

I sit down in the chair next to her bed, take her hand and ask, "How are you?"

"Feeling old," she replies with a smile.

"We have done interesting things," I say.

"More than interesting. Exceptional."

After we moved to New York, Jill went to medical school while I traded stocks in the morning and went to acting school in the afternoon. After she finished her studies, we were married.

Louie and Sue moved here, and the four of us lived together for a time until we purchased the larger six-bedroom apartment next door.

We hired private jets, and the four of us traveled the world, always attempting to stay away from crowds. While Eleni was living, we went back to Patmos every year to see her, as I had promised. That was always a time to reconnect with John's book.

In fact, exploring John's book revealed that there is much more than thinking and growing rich. I learned to not let the making of wealth become an obsessive goal, for there were more important things in life, like Jill and family. Most important, and above everything, is the immaculate being on the throne, and responding to His faithfulness.

It takes me a moment to remember what Jill said. I reflect on her comment and respond, "I don't know what exceptional is."

She chuckles. "I understand. Exceptional is a value judgment, and sometimes that's ambiguous for you. All I can confirm is that you helped people along the way. I like that."

"It's because of you," I tell her. "You helped me help people," I say that knowing that caring for people is not customary for me because of my condition.

"You encouraged some people to make good life choices," she says.

"Do you mean because I told them of their future?"

"Yes. That put many people on a good track, although some didn't accept what you revealed to them."

"I know. Those people chose to go down the black river, only to crash over the waterfall into an eternity without light."

"Arlo, your descriptions never cease to amaze me. You also helped people financially, starting with your own family."

"I had few feelings for that. You gave me guidance." Jill could identify needs in people. That was too complicated for me, for my abilities were narrow. I had little knowledge about the good and the bad of giving money, unless someone like Jill helped me.

If anything, my helping of people came from logic, and in seeing the rivers of their histories. But maybe some decisions didn't have logic. For instance, Louie wanted to keep the orange farm, and I wanted to protect the oak tree. For some, that might not make sense, but that's what we did. Carlos ran the farm, and he brought his family up from Mexico to be with him.

"You helped more than your family," Jill says. "Many others benefited from your support."

"That's only because of you," I reply. "For me, it is simple to think and grow rich. Knowing how best to help people is too problematical."

"That's why we are a good team," Jill says.

"I know. I see harmonious colors when I am with you. We complement each other. You have compassion in the present, and I see the future."

Jill takes a deep breath. "Yes, you definitely see the future." Her soft blue eyes look at me, and she asks, "How much time do I have left?"

"Not much. Maybe one or two days."

She smiles. "I always liked your honesty." She takes a deep breath and looks beyond me, as though she is peering at something in the sky. She says, "Death is a wonderful thing. It puts reality on the table."

"Why's that?" I ask.

"Humans believe they are gods, but death is a way of

confirming they are not."

"For sure," I respond, for that makes logical sense. "What about the crystal city?"

Jill gives a tired grin. "That I do believe in. We have seen the inauguration of that kingdom over our years together."

She sounds like me. I say, "Then someday I will meet you there."

"Yes, you shall," she states. After a deep breath, Jill says, "I love you Arlo and thank you for your love and kindness to me over the years."

"I love you too." I can confirm this, even knowing that love is an emotion I don't experience like others. Instead, her pink and pastel hues are unique, and I attribute my reaction to her inimitable characteristics as love. She has been caring for me all my life. When our colors blend so harmoniously, it confirms she is the love of my life.

Jill shuts her eyes and falls asleep, so I quietly stand up from the chair and bend over and kiss her on her forehead. Then I sway, take my cane, and walk toward the door. Turning around, I see a pearly white mist forming above her. It's the same mist that was above my grandfather and Maria and Louie and Sue and my mother.

For a while I watch it hover above Jill. It's not yet touching her. I leave the room. I will come back before it does.

* * *

I go back to the window and look at the city and see the world. History is going somewhere, each decision and event taking a position in the purposeful flow of time. I can accurately predict the future, not all of it but some of it. This forecasting started the day I fell out of the oak tree.

* * *

But later on, I had another significant experience at the oak tree. It happened the day Jill drove us from San Diego to our orange farm in her new Corvette car. After we arrived at the farm, and after I showed her around, she left me alone in front of the tree.

Standing there my knees trembled, and with a shaking hand I reached past the electrical impulses and touched the tree. The bark was hard, and it made me remember the hurt on the day of the fall.

With my hand on the tree, I glanced down to the ground and saw the large rock, where I hit my head and lost consciousness.

Since that fall, the oak tree had been two contradictory forces. At times it was my friend, a protector, a teacher, and a guide. Occasionally on my journey, it had appeared as a symbol of support.

Yet, there was an opposing power. The tree was my antagonist, a force filling me with fear. At least, in my world of limited emotions, that's how I interpreted the colors and electrical tentacles extending from the tree. Fear.

And, because of that fear, the oak tree reigned over me. Most likely it came from the terrible pain when I fell, a profound shock to my inner being.

I imagined that's how it is with regular people. When there is a deep trauma, whether emotional or physical, it can control them and limit them for many years to come.

What I needed, if possible, was to overcome the fearful part of the tree, to remove the power it held over me. It would be debilitating to carry that burden for the rest of my life without dealing with it. To conquer this was of primary importance, but it seemed a hopeless task.

With a quivering body, I reached up, took hold of a branch and sensed its strength. Then, I pulled myself up and stood on it.

My legs wobbled, and I waited a moment, wondering if I had done the right thing. Then, I reached higher to another branch and then another, my hands and feet going up from one branch to the next.

The tree emitted warning signals that I shouldn't be there. The brownish-green leaves sent a memory flash of the slow-motion movie of my fall, and how those prickly leaves passed in front of my eyes.

After that fall, I saw the world differently. After that, spoken words became colors and streams. After that, I could predict the outcomes of horse races and stock markets and people and history.

Yet the fall from the tree was a painful shock, and I remembered how my ribs and head felt, and the dizziness that stayed for days.

That dizziness returned when I was halfway up the tree, and the universe screamed at me to turn around and go back down. Yet, I was not the kind of person to deviate from a goal once it had been set.

I glanced down at the large rock patiently waiting, realizing that another fall might kill me. But, that reality was of secondary importance.

I pressed on.

Slowly I moved up, and the branches became smaller. Then I had the memory of the pistol shot sound of a branch breaking.

I moved with caution.

The central trunk was solid, and it supported my weight.

Finally, I reached the top of the tree, breathing deeply, my heart beating fast.

At the top of the tree, I fixed my feet against two branches and held on to the most stable branch that extended upward from the tree trunk.

This was the final task I had determined on the island of

Patmos. It was to set me free from the tree's controlling power.

Now I could move freely toward my goals without this encumbrance. Things needed to be accomplished, and many brilliant experiences waited in the future.

Most important was Jill, for she was not a thing, but a person. I was fourteen, and she was eighteen, almost nineteen. I was comfortable with her, but it was much more than that. I wanted to be with her forever. She waited for me at our farmhouse, although, I required a bit more time on my own.

Lifting my eyes, I scanned across the tops of the orange trees to the farthest horizon and had an eternal view of the world.

ABOUT THE AUTHOR

To learn more about Cass Tell and his books, go to his website.

There you will also find reader-group questions for
The SAVANT.

www.casstell.com

CPSIA information can be obtained
at www.ICGtesting.com
Printed in the USA
BVHW082039300619
552298BV00002B/306/P